Julien Gracq

Abounding Freedom

translated from French by Alice Yang

 WORLD POETRY

Abounding Freedom by Julien Gracq
Copyright © Éditions Corti, 1946, 1958, 1969, 1970
(Original title: *Liberté grande*)
English translation copyright © Alice Yang, 2024
Introduction copyright © Alice Yang, 2024

First Edition, First Printing, 2024
ISBN 978-1-954218-22-2

World Poetry Books
New York, NY
www.worldpoetrybooks.com

Distributed in the US by SPD/Small Press Distribution
www.spdbooks.org

Distributed in the UK and Europe by Turnaround Publisher Services
www.turnaround-uk.com

Library of Congress Control Number: 2024930183

Cover design by Andrew Bourne
Typesetting by Don't Look Now
Printed in Lithuania by BALTO Print

World Poetry Books publishes exceptional translations of poetry from a broad
range of languages and traditions, bringing the work of modern masters, emerging
voices, and pioneering innovators from around the world to English-language
readers in affordable trade editions. Founded in 2017, World Poetry Books is
a 501(c)(3) nonprofit and charitable organization based in New York City and
affiliated with the Translation Program and the Humanities Institute at the
University of Connecticut (Storrs).

UCONN
HUMANITIES INSTITUTE

Table of Contents

Introduction

FAME AND RECOGNITION SEEMED TO come Julien Gracq's way despite himself. A recluse, he often criticized the literary establishment and famously refused the Prix Goncourt in 1951 for his third novel, *The Opposing Shore*—a gesture that ironically propelled him further into public view. Still, Gracq kept a low profile and avoided the mainstream literary world, continuing to write and publish with the small press José Corti throughout his life, even as Gallimard made multiple attempts to court him. Perhaps his greatest honor, the only one he seems to have accepted, was the inclusion of his complete works in the Bibliothèque de la Pléiade, a distinction just a handful of authors have enjoyed while still alive. Julien Gracq is, in short, something of a quiet titan in French letters.

He wasn't destined to become a writer. Or, rather, Louis Poirier wasn't destined to become the writer Julien Gracq. Born in 1910 to a family of shopkeepers in the small town of Saint-Florent-le-Vieil, Poirier was a precocious child who excelled in school. While he chose to study geography at the École Normale Supérieure and the Institut d'Études Politiques (Sciences Po) in Paris, he also developed an interest in contemporary literature. André Breton's "First Manifesto of Surrealism" and *Nadja*, along with several other seminal Surrealist texts, came to him as a revelation: "I felt like a door had opened onto unexplored domains, or merely glimpsed domains, of poetry."

It would take nearly another decade—spent finishing his studies, taking on various teaching posts, and serving in the military—for Poirier to pursue writing seriously. In 1939, he published his first book, *The Castle of Argol*. So began his life as the author Julien Gracq, a pen name he chose in part for its sonority and brevity. The first name pays homage to Julien Sorel, the protagonist of one of his favorite novels, Stendhal's *The Red and the Black*, while the last refers to the Gracchi

brothers, social reformers of the Roman Republic. Though *The Castle of Argol* initially received little attention, it found a vocal advocate in Breton, who praised it as the first Surrealist novel. The two writers met shortly after the book's publication and went on to develop a profound literary and personal rapport. Despite his close relationship with Breton, however, Gracq was averse to the collective activity of the Surrealist movement and never considered himself a member of the group.

Just as Gracq was garnering attention for his writing, the Second World War began and put his literary and professional careers on hold. As a lieutenant, he served in various cities in France and Holland before the Germans took him as prisoner in 1940. He was released a year later, after contracting an illness suspected (wrongly) to be tuberculosis. Upon his return to France, Gracq went back to teaching, started a PhD in geography, then abandoned his studies because he found the work tedious. In 1947, he landed a permanent position as *professeur agrégé* of geography and history at the Lycée Claude Bernard in Paris, where he taught until his retirement in 1970.

With Gracq's return from the war came a spurt of literary production, including his second novel, *A Dark Stranger*, and a critical study, *André Breton. Quelques aspects de l'écrivain* (*André Breton: A Few Aspects of the Writer*), published in 1945 and 1948, respectively. By the time he published his fourth and final novel, *Balcony in the Forest*, in 1958, his literary reputation had been secured, in part due to the Prix Goncourt affair. He shifted then to writing essays and prose fragments that mixed memoir, travel writing, and reflections on literature, and remained in these genres until his death in 2007.

In addition to novels and nonfiction, Gracq produced a sole book of prose poetry: *Abounding Freedom*. The first edition, published in 1946, included the forty poems he wrote from 1941–43, just after his release from German captivity. In 1958 a second edition appeared containing eight additional poems

written in the late forties and fifties, six of which were gathered under the title "The Habitable Earth." A third edition, which included a final poem—"Aubrac," written in 1963—came out a decade later.

Because Gracq composed them over such a long period of time, these poems offer a window into the evolution of his style. The early poems recall the frenetic energy of the Surrealist ethos, teeming with surprising, disorienting, and logic-defying descriptions, metaphors, similes, syntax, and juxtapositions of words. Gracq's dense style in these early pieces further destabilizes his prose poetry: images, phrases, and appositions accumulate to vertiginous effect. This stems in part from the "abounding freedom" he found in writing poetry, a form that allowed him to let his pen, as he put it, "run its course."

Such a method might at first glance resemble automatic writing, but Gracq rejected this classification, likely because it suggested, in theory, an unedited stream of the unconscious. (In practice, the Surrealists often reworked pieces of so-called automatic writing.) Indeed, Gracq took care to revise his poems, some more than others, and, to all appearances, sought to heighten the strangeness of his original drafts. Consider, for instance, this excerpt of "Grand Hotel," which centers on its setting's luxury and extravagance:

> I'd be doing a disservice to luxury by sparing it those tasteless details that mysteriously poeticize it: summer furs, melancholy cascades of change ringing along staircases of gravestones, smoking parlors with plumed voices dazed by cordovan leathers, nickel bars of railings from which the horizon flees toward the piers.

Incompatible elements proliferate: "summer furs," "staircases of gravestones," "plumed voices," "nickel bars," as opposed to zinc bars, and the horizon that "flees toward the piers," rather

than away from them. Tellingly, an early draft shows that, of those five phrases, Gracq added contrary elements to three in revising the poem. "Staircases of gravestones" was originally "gala staircases," "plumed voices" simply "voices," and "nickel bars" simply "bars." Gracq was consciously creating a world of inconsistencies.

This effort to destabilize also emerges on a macroscopic level. "Worldly Scandals," for instance, comprises three unrelated poems first composed as separate stand-alone pieces. He matched titles with poems in seemingly arbitrary fashion: "The Good Inn" was initially entitled "Parties at the House of Augustulus," which itself was previously called "The Valley of Josaphat," which became the title of another poem in the collection. This method of juxtaposition, collage, and shuffling is emblematic of Gracq's enterprise: by combining apparently disparate elements, he expands the interpretive possibilities and intensifies the strangeness of his poetry.

This practice aligns him with Rimbaud, the great precursor of Surrealism. Indeed, we can consider the first edition of *Abounding Freedom* the *Illuminations* of Gracq's oeuvre; in its density of images, each poem is an illumination, an engraved illustration and flash of inspiration. The essence of Rimbaud's poems, as described by his close friend the essayist Ernest Delahaye, helps shed light on Gracq's own poetry:

> Rimbaud is hardly looking to "invent." A categorical partisan of observation, he often takes real things that he has known then displaces them from their tried and true combinations, divides them into usable parts with new meanings, gathers and unites details that were once far apart, strips a given subject of its property in order to give it to another, etc.

We have seen that Gracq, like Rimbaud, creates striking juxtapositions. What Delahaye reminds us is that those

juxtapositions are grounded in reality. Gracq himself expresses a similar sentiment to Delahaye's: "in a work said to be of the imagination, memory plays no less a role than in a realist work ... all the elements are furnished—they're simply recomposed in a different way." There is nothing fantastical about Gracq's poems; he merely presents reality in an unexpected light.

Even so, the accumulation of discordant elements often makes it difficult to visualize a composite tableau in a given poem, to piece together its individual parts. Rather than seek a logical unity, we should understand each poem as what Maurice Blanchot called, in a review of *A Dark Stranger*, an "indistinct whole, a disorganized world of things." Each poem creates an impression of the whole, but its discrete parts—words, phrases, or sentences—don't necessarily add up in a neat or immediately comprehensible manner. What holds these parts together is the way Gracq's sentences flow into each other. He was highly attuned to rhythm and sound, arranging words and syntax to please the ear.

Like his Symbolist predecessors—especially Rimbaud, whose ironic prose poem "City" is quoted in the epigraph to *Abounding Freedom*—Gracq was ambivalent toward urban settings. In some poems, the city offers a source of possibility and poetic inspiration; in others, it gives way to a sense of alienation. The poet is often confronted with the limits of a city, which he attempts to transcend by reimagining his urban surroundings or by taking to the ring roads, the outskirts, the liminal space between the city and the countryside. Gracq's continual drift toward such in-between spaces reflects his predilection for abandoned areas where nature and decay seem to overtake man-made creations—as at "the edges of provincial towns ... the sudden introduction of neighborhoods with disused factories" ("Hanging Gardens"). Temporal interstices also frame many of his poems, such as the time one spends

waiting, the build-up to a climactic event, or transitional times of day like dawn and dusk.

Seascapes, too, proliferate in Gracq's poems. The boat drifting at sea provides the ultimate metaphor for the imagination. And just as one may have endless ways to navigate the imagination, Gracq alludes to a delightfully extensive range of boats: scows, wherries, pleasure boats, three-masted windjammers, and tartans, to name a few. Maritime terms appear constantly, a testament to Gracq's love of obscure words and references that require special knowledge to understand, particularly knowledge of architecture, history, and, above all, geography.

Indeed, place names—both esoteric and well known—are scattered throughout the collection, whether in similes or as launching points for Gracq's associative drift. "Susquehanna River," for instance, begins at the eponymous river, only to evoke "Dutch embankments" in the very first sentence before snaking through a series of disparate images. Gracq often associates geographical locations with women. In "Transbaikalia," the rivers Nonni, Kherlen, and Selenga offer the basis for his descriptions of a lover. "River," after all, is feminine in French (*la rivière*), as are the words for "city" (*la ville*) and "sea" (*la mer*).

Women appear elsewhere throughout the collection as well, not just as lovers and analogues to places, but also as figures of authority and defiance. "Unattainable," for instance, describes a woman as an author: her hand is likened to a "plume," while her gait writes its "mysterious print between asphalt margins," just as a pen writes between the margins of a piece of paper. And in her authorial power, Gracq writes, she can rival a *"littérateur"*—a man of letters.

The later poems published in the second and third editions of *Abounding Freedom* echo some of the earlier poems' common threads—difficult images, an interest in place, long and intricate sentences. Yet they also give way to a different poetic sensibility, one that doesn't pulse with quite the same energy.

They take smaller leaps in their associative logic and savor an imaginative realm in a more sustained fashion. They're more serene, subdued, controlled, and grounded. Memories surface more strongly than before: "Siesta in Dutch Flanders," "Gomorrah," and "Aubrac" are explicitly based on concrete events in Gracq's life. If the earlier poems show him rearranging elements of reality, the later ones do, too, though with a greater degree of verisimilitude and nostalgia.

Apart from "Paris at Dawn," the setting of these later poems is always natural rather than urban, a shift that indicates an increasing desire to capture what Gracq called the "human plant," which he defined as the "assured, insoluble union ... between man and the world that holds him." The poet is a plant that inhabits the world; the mind lets go of all tension and seamlessly blends into the natural surroundings: "At the heart of the dissolving night, all cables cut, all weights cast off, surrendering to the air and carried on water, I was a pure vessel of exchange and communion" ("The Uplands of Sertalejo"). Rather than drift in his imagination—like the metaphorical boats at sea in his earlier poems—Gracq now drifts, "carried on water," in his natural surroundings. As the writer Gilles Plazy put it, "the poet no longer dreams of the world, he inhabits it"—a reflection of the title that gathers the first six of these additional poems: "The Habitable Earth."

"The Road," which I've translated as a coda in the present edition, is a fragment of an unfinished novel Gracq started in 1953. He worked on the book for three years before putting it aside, struggling to define a narrative structure for his imagined setting: an invaded country abandoned to nature. The piece Gracq eventually published as "The Road" in 1963 consists of two entries from the diary that was to frame the novel. (The entire unfinished manuscript was published posthumously in 2014.) Despite the first-person account, the prose is strangely impersonal in its extensive, precise descriptions of

the eponymous road and its travelers. Such narrative self-efface-
ment adds to the mythic quality of the piece, which evokes a
world that seems to exist paradoxically in history and outside
of time. In its style, themes, and atmosphere, "The Road" of-
fers a bridge between Gracq's prose poems and his novels *The
Opposing Shore* and *Balcony in the Forest*. Indeed, Gracq aban-
doned "The Road" to write the latter, whose setting during the
"phony war" represents the concrete source of the mysterious
withdrawal from life that haunts the fragment.

* * *

IN THE TRANSLATIONS THAT FOLLOW, I sought to preserve the
characteristic length of Gracq's winding sentences, though I've
sometimes taken syntactic liberties to recreate the sonority of
his prose. The original French version of "Unattainable," for
instance, contains the anaphoric use of *quel* in an extended
rhetorical question. The literal translation "which" or "what"
would have weighed down the English, so the question
in English becomes a declarative sentence with "no" as the
anaphoric device.

As for diction, I've generally avoided cognates that would
create semantic, rhythmic, or sonic interference. The title pro-
vides a case in point: *Liberté grande*, which could be literally
rendered as *Great Liberty*. To my ear, *Abounding Freedom* effec-
tively captures the sense of opening in the original title. The
drawn-out diphthong in "abounding" echoes in its way the
long nasal vowel of *grande*. When it came to technical words,
however, I often opted for literal translations to maintain
the strangeness of the original. I didn't want to gloss terms
like *échauguette* or *élytres*, which French readers would be un-
likely to know, and rendered them with the equally obscure

"bartizan," a turret projecting from a fortress, and "elytra," the protective forewings of certain insects.

Gracq sought to write what he once called "practically untranslatable" prose. In other words, he aimed—as many French poets did—to create a language almost entirely of his own. To that end, he developed a dense, lyrical style that runs throughout his prose poetry and poetic prose alike, even as his sensibility evolved over time. In *Abounding Freedom*, expansive imaginative realms, surprising images, and a spellbinding sense of suspension arise from Gracq's artfully worked sentences. It's the sonority and linguistic tension of those sentences that have led me with pleasure through my repeated readings of these poems and that, above all, I've tried to capture in these pages.

—*Alice Yang*

Abounding Freedom

Je suis un éphémère et point trop mécontent ci-
toyen d'une métropole crue moderne parce que tout
goût connu a été éludé dans les ameublements et
l'extérieur des maisons aussi bien que dans le plan
de la ville. Ici vous ne signaleriez les traces d'aucun
monument de superstition.

Rimbaud, *Les Illuminations*

I am an ephemeral and not at all dissatisfied citizen of a metropolis thought to be modern because every known taste has been avoided in the furnishings and exteriors of its houses as well as in the plan of the city. Here you would never point to the traces of any monument to superstition.

Rimbaud, *Illuminations*
(trans. John Ashbery)

Pour galvaniser l'urbanisme

Gêné que je suis toujours, sur les lisières d'une ville où cependant il serait pour nous d'une telle séduction de voir par exemple les beaux chiendents des steppes friser au pied même de l'extravagante priapée des gratte-ciel, déçu par le dégradé avilissant, la visqueuse matière interstitielle des banlieues, et, sur les plans, leurs cancéreuses auréoles, je rêve depuis peu d'une Ville qui s'ouvrît, tranchée net comme par l'outil, et pour ainsi dire saignante d'un vif sang noir d'asphalte à toutes ses artères coupées, sur la plus grasse, la plus abandonnée, la plus secrète des campagnes bocagères. Que ne pourrait-on espérer d'une ville, féminine entre toutes, qui consentît, sur l'autel d'une solitaire préoccupation esthétique, le sacrifice de cet embonpoint, moins pléthorique encore que gangreneux, où s'empêtre perversement comme dans les bouffissures de l'enfance la beauté la plus mûre et la plus glorieuse d'avoir été fatiguée par les siècles, le visage d'une grande cité. Le papillon sorti du cocon brillant des couleurs du rêve pour la plus courte, je le veux bien, la plus condamnée des existences, c'est à peine s'il donnerait l'idée de cette fantastique vision du vaisseau de Paris prêt à larguer ses amarres pour un voyage au fond même du songe, et secouant avec la vermine de sa coque le *rémore* inévitable, les câbles et les étais pourris des Servitudes Économiques. Oui, même oubliée la salle où l'on projetait l'Age d'Or, il pourrait être spécialement agréable, terminée la représentation de quelque Vaisseau Fantôme, de poser sur le perron de l'Opéra un pied distrait et pour une fois à peine surpris par la caresse de l'herbe fraîche, d'écouter percer derrière les orages marins du théâtre la cloche d'une *vraie* vache, et de ne s'étonner que

Toward Urban Galvanization

Uneasy as I always am, at the edges of a city where it would, however, seduce us to see, for instance, the lovely couch-grass of the steppes grazing the foot of the extravagant erection of skyscrapers, disappointed by the deteriorating gradation, the viscous, interstitial matter of the suburbs, and, on the maps, their cancerous halos, I've recently dreamt of a City that opens, cut cleanly as though by a tool and bleeding, so to speak, the lively black blood of asphalt from all of its severed arteries, onto the most fertile, most deserted, most secluded land of a wooded country. What couldn't one hope of a city, feminine above all, that agreed, on the altar of a single aesthetic concern, to the sacrifice of that excess weight, not so much plethoric as gangrenous, which perversely enmeshes the face of a large city, as childhood puffiness does the most magnificent beauty matured by the centuries. The butterfly, brilliant with the colors of dreams, having emerged from its cocoon to live the briefest and, I'd say, the most ill-fated of existences, would hardly evoke the idea of that fanciful vision of Paris as a vessel ready to cast off for a journey into the very depths of a dream and, with the vermin of its hull, shaking off the unavoidable *remoras*, the cables and rotten stays of Economic Servitude. Yes, regardless of the theater where *The Golden Age* was shown, it might be particularly pleasant, at the end of the performance of some Phantom Ship, to set down a distracted foot, for once scarcely surprised by the caress of fresh grass, on the front steps of the Opera, to listen, over the theater's sea storms, to the piercing bell of a *real* cow, and to be startled only slightly that a rustic gallop, begun between the pillars, suddenly makes ruffled charges shrink into the endless

vaguement qu'une galopade rustique, commencée entre les piliers, soudain fasse rapetisser à l'infini comme par un truc de scène des coursiers échevelés sur un océan *vert prairie* plus réussi que nature.

Serais-je le seul ? Je songe maintenant à ce goût panoramique du contraste, à ce choix du dépouillement dans le site où s'édifieront les constructions les plus superflues, les plus abandonnées au luxe, palaces de skieurs, caravansérails, dancings des déserts, des Saharas, des pics à glaciers, où trouve à s'avouer avec naïveté je ne sais quel besoin moderne d'ironie et d'érémitisme. Revient surtout me hanter cette phrase d'un poème de Rimbaud, que sans doute j'interprète si mal — à ma manière : « Ce soir, à Circeto des hautes glaces... ». J'imagine, dans un décor capable à lui seul de proscrire toute idée simplement galante, ce rendez-vous solennel et sans lendemain. Au-dessus de vallées plus abruptes, plus profondes, plus noires que la nuit polaire, de culminations énormes de montagnes serrées dans la nuit épaule contre épaule sous leur pèlerine de forêts — comme dans la « pyramide humaine » au-dessus des nuques de jeunes Atlas raidis par l'effort une gracieuse apparition, bras étendus, semble s'envoler sur la pointe d'un seul pied — , ou plus encore comme à la lueur du jour la céleste Visitation des neiges éternelles, leur attouchement à chaque cime de gloire dans une lumière de Pentecôte — l'œil dressé sous un angle impossible perçoit en plein ciel d'hiver nocturne des phares tournoyants dans les sarabandes de la neige, de splendides et longues voitures glissant sans bruit le long des avenues balayées, où parfois un glacier dénude familièrement la blancheur incongrue d'une épaule énorme — et toutes pleines de jouets somptueux, d'enfants calmes, de profondes fourrures, et se hâtant tout au long des interminables et nobles façades des palais d'*hiver* vers la Noël mystérieuse et nostalgique de cette capitale des glaces.

horizon, as though by a trick of scenery, on a *meadow-green* ocean more convincing than nature.

Might I be the only one? I think now of that panoramic taste for contrast, that choice of starkness in the site where the most superfluous of constructions will arise, the most given to luxury, ski resorts, caravansaries, dance halls in deserts, Saharas, glacier peaks, where who knows what modern need of irony and reclusiveness manages to expose itself naively. A phrase from a poem of Rimbaud's, which I may be misinterpreting, comes back to haunt me in particular—the way I have it: "This evening, to Circeto of the tall ice ..." I imagine, in a setting inclined to reject any merely gallant idea, this solemn and short-lived encounter. Above valleys steeper, darker, deeper than the polar night, above enormous culminations of mountains packed shoulder to shoulder beneath their cloak of forests at night—as in the "human pyramid," above the napes of young Atlases tense from stress, a gracious apparition, arms spread, seems to take flight from the tip of her toe—or else in the gleaming day, the celestial visitation of eternal snow fondling every glorious peak in a Pentecost light—from an impossible angle, one raises one's eyes and perceives, in the winter's open night sky, swirling headlights in the sarabands of snow, splendid and long cars silently gliding along the swept avenues, where sometimes a glacier casually reveals the conspicuous whiteness of an enormous shoulder—cars full of sumptuous toys, calm children, thick fur coats, rushing past the endless, noble facades of the *winter* palaces toward the mysterious, nostalgic Christmas of this ice capital.

The charming memory I've kept of that city where pink flares dazzled in the snowy hills, where, at midnight, the *jeunesse dorée* of rich neighborhoods threw flaming torches into the abyss surrounding this frozen belvedere, watching them vanish slowly and steadily into the black transparency, until, gasping from a slight sense of nausea, they looked up at the

Le souvenir charmant que j'ai gardé de cette ville où les feux de bengale roses éclataient dans les collines de neige, où la jeunesse dorée des quartiers riches, à minuit, s'amusait à jeter dans les précipices qui ceinturent ce belvédère de glace des torches enflammées qui rapetissaient mollement, régulièrement, dans la transparence noire, jusqu'à ce que, le souffle coupé par une nausée vague, on relevât les yeux vers la nuit piquetée d'étoiles froides, et qu'on sentît la planète pivoter sur cette extrême pointe. Devant le perron du casino, deux avenues immaculées, escarpées, majestueuses, entrecroisaient une courbe à double évolution ; lancées comme dans un toboggan, moteur calé, des voitures en ramenaient, vers les jolies banlieues verticales, les derniers fêtards sur le rythme doux des aérolithes, la lumière électrique, si pauvre toujours et si grelottante sur les rues blanches, je l'ai vue s'enrichir de sous-entendus d'au-delà, de magnifiques points d'orgue à chaque pli de la neige, plus suspecte et plus que les plaines de toutes les Russies lourde, pouvait-on croire, de cadavres de contrebande sous cet éclairage pestilentiel.

Mais, à quatre heures du matin, dans l'air glacé, les immenses avenues vides sous leurs lumières clignotantes ! Une brume vague montait des abîmes, et, complice de la somnolence du froid extrême, mêlait les étoiles aux lumières infimes de la vallée. Accoudé à un parapet de pierre, l'œil aux gouffres frais et nuageux, humides au matin comme une bouche, ma rêverie enfin prenait un sens. Sur les kilomètres vertigineux de ces avenues démesurées, on n'entendait plus que le bruissement des lampes à arc et les craquements secs des glaciers tout proches, comme une bête qui secoue sa chaîne dans la nuit. Parfois, au bout d'une perspective, un ivrogne enjambait la rampe d'un boulevard extérieur comme un bastingage.

Villes ! — trop mollement situées !

Et pourtant, des villes réelles, une me toucherait encore jusqu'à l'exaltation : je veux parler de Saint-Nazaire. Sur une

night sky studded with cold stars and sensed the planet pivoting on this extreme point. In front of the casino steps, two immaculate, steep, majestic avenues crisscrossed with a bend; thrown as though down a slide, their engines stalled, cars cruised toward the lovely, perpendicular suburbs, bringing back the last partygoers on the soft rhythm of aerolites. I saw that electric light, always so faint and wavering on the white streets, enriched with hints from beyond, with magnificent fermatas at every fold of snow, more suspect and covered, it seemed, with more contraband corpses than all of Russia's fields under that pestilent lighting.

But at four in the morning, in the chilly air, the immense empty avenues under their flickering lights! A faint mist rose from the depths and, complicit with the drowsiness of the extreme cold, blended the stars with the valley's dim lights. My elbow against a stone parapet, eyes like cool, cloudy chasms damp as a mouth in the morning air, my reverie was finally taking on meaning. Over the dizzying kilometers of these endless avenues, the only sounds that could be heard were the hum of arc lights and the sharp crunch of snow on nearby glaciers, like the rattle of an animal's chain at night. Sometimes, in the distance, a drunkard stepped over the ramp of an outer boulevard as if it were a railing.

Cities!—all too carelessly situated!

And yet, of all these real cities, one could still move me to the point of exaltation: I mean Saint-Nazaire. On low ground, swept by the sea ahead, eaten away by the swamps behind it, the city is hardly—thrown onto this mown grass which, like an animal's sheen of fur, accentuates the vigorous limbs of Brittany's coast—but a herd of white and gray houses, clumsily dispersed like sheep on a heath, though denser in the center, as if huddled together over the common fear of gales from the sea. What's rather tragic are the outskirts of this city, which I've always thought poorly anchored to the ground, prone to

terre basse, balayée devant par la mer, minée derrière par les marais, elle n'est guère — jetées sur ce gazon ras qui fait valoir comme le poil lustré d'une bête la membrure vigoureuse des côtes bretonnes — , qu'un troupeau de maisons blanches et grises, maladroitement semées comme des moutons sur la lande, mais plus denses au centre, et comme agglutinées par la peur des grands coups de vent de mer. Assez tragique est l'abord de cette ville, que je me suis toujours imaginée mal ancrée au sol, prête à céder à je ne sais quelle dérive sournoise. Des boqueteaux de grues géantes aux bras horizontaux se lèvent comme des pinèdes pardessus les berges boueuses, en migration perpétuelle, de ce grand fleuve gris du nord appelant comme une rédemption la blancheur des cygnes de légende qu'est devenue dans un mélancolique avatar final la rivière lumineuse et molle de la Touraine.

Par la vitre du wagon, on songe aussi, pris dans le champ d'un périscope, au camp d'atterrissage des géants martiens à tripodes de Wells.

Je lui dus, par un bel été, la surprise d'une de ces poétiques collusions, de ces *drôles d'idées* qui naissent parfois aux choses et laissent soudain interdite la pire fantaisie. Pardessus les toits de ses maisons basses, la ville, en moquerie profonde, je pense, de ses dérisoires attaches terrestres, avait hissé en guise de *nef* de sa cathédrale absente — haute de trente mètres et visible mieux que les clochers de Chartres à dix lieues à la ronde, la coque énorme entre ses tins du paquebot « Normandie ». Ville glissant de partout à la mer comme sa voguante cathédrale de tôle, ville où je me suis senti le plus parfaitement, sur le vague boulevard de brumes qui domine le large, entre les belles géographies sur l'asphalte d'une averse matinale et tôt séchée, dériver comme la gabare sans mâts du poète sous son doux ciel aventureux.

Mais ce Saint-Nazaire que je rêve du fond de ma chambre existe-t-il encore ? Lui et tant d'autres. Villes impossibles

give way to who knows what deviating drift. Copses of giant cranes with horizontal arms, in perpetual migration, rise like pines over the muddy banks of this northern gray river calling forth, as though in search of redemption, the whiteness of magic swans which, in a final melancholy reincarnation, is what has become of the gentle, luminous river of Touraine.

Through the window of the train car, one also thinks of the landing camp, caught in a periscope's field of view, of Wells's giant Martians with their tripods.

I was indebted to him, one fine summer, for the surprise of one of those poetic collusions, one of those *funny ideas* that sometimes come into being and suddenly preclude the worst of fantasies. Over the roofs of its low houses, the city—out of profound mockery, I believe, of its absurd attachments to the ground—had hoisted, in lieu of the *nave* of its absent cathedral, the enormous hull of the liner Normandie between its keel blocks—30 meters tall and more visible than the bell towers of Chartres from ten leagues away. A city gliding from all points to the sea, like its sailing iron cathedral, a city where I felt most acutely that—on the faint, misty boulevard overlooking the expanse, between the asphalt's lovely maps etched by a quickly dried morning shower—I was drifting like a poet's mastless scow under his sweet adventurous sky.

But does it still exist, this Saint-Nazaire I dream up from the depths of my bedroom? It does, and so do many more. Impossible cities, like those built by opium, with smooth glacial facades, silent cobblestones, pediments lost in the clouds, De Quincey's cities and Baudelaire's, Broadways of dreams with dizzying slices of granite—de Chirico's hypnotized cities—built by Amphion's harp, destroyed by Jericho's trumpet—in all of time, wasn't it recorded in the most moving of fables that your stones, hanging from the strings of a lyre, needed only the slightest poetic inspiration to start into motion? I'd like to entrust this myth, which so clearly suggests

comme celles que bâtit l'opium, aux lisses façades glacia-
les, aux pavés muets, aux frontons perdus dans les nuages,
villes de Quincey et de Baudelaire, Broadways du rêve aux
vertigineuses tranchées de granit — villes hypnotisées de
Chirico — bâties par la harpe d'Amphion, détruites par la
trompette de Jéricho — de tout temps ne fut-il pas inscrit
dans la plus touchante des fables que vos pierres, suspendues
aux cordes de la lyre, n'attendaient jamais, pour se mettre en
mouvement, que les plus fragiles inspirations de la poésie.
C'est à ce mythe qui fait dépendre, avec combien de lucidité,
du souffle le plus pur de l'esprit la remise en question des
sujétions les plus accablantes de la pesanteur que je voudrais
confier les secrets espoirs que je continue à nourrir de n'être
pas éternellement prisonnier de telle sordide rue de boutiques
qu'il m'est donné (!) par exemple d'habiter en ce moment.

Pourquoi ne m'accrocherais-je pas à de telles pensées pour
me donner le cœur de sourire parfois de leurs villes de pierres
et de briques ? Libre à eux de croire s'y *loger*. Le diable après
tout n'y perd rien et, tout boiteux qu'il est, paraît-il, comme la
justice, n'aura jamais fini d'en faire sauter les toits.

that the spirit's purest breath can defy gravity's most oppressive constraints, with the secret hopes I continue to nourish of not being eternally prisoner to some sordid shop-lined street, where I happen (!) to be living now.

Why shouldn't I cling to such thoughts that make me smile, now and then, at their cities of stone and brick? My hopes are free to believe themselves *lodged* there. The devil, after all, can't be fooled, and though he seems to limp, like justice, he'll never stop blowing up rooftops.

Venise

Sur cette plage où la neige volait de conserve avec de légères frondaisons d'écume, aux rayons du soleil de cinq heures, je sonnais à la grille du palais Martinengo. J'étais seul au centre géométrique de ce gigantesque haussement d'un sourcil de sable — encore quelques minutes et les dunes sonnant la retraite allaient me barrer le passage des vagues de leurs blonds escadrons. La sonnerie pénétrait comme un quatorze juillet de pétards et de drapeaux des corridors somnolents comme de l'huile, des galeries de bronze aux dérisoires armures de pacotille, dérangeait sous un repli d'ombre le coffre aux trésors. Le bois de pins, derrière, était tout à coup semblable à la lumière minérale des projecteurs, quand l'orchestre prélude au clair de lune de *Werther*. C'était bien, je pouvais me le dire avec ravissement, la solitude. Au-dessus de moi claquait au vent, solennel comme un portant de théâtre, le volet d'une haute fenêtre au milieu d'une galopade de sable. La mer tonnante d'un bout à l'autre de la baie raccourcissait l'issue d'une escapade douteuse. De la main gauche je cherchais à briser le plus délicatement possible la vitre d'un de ces charmants coffrets du XVIIIe où se dissimule parfois la bouche d'un avertisseur d'incendie. Le spectacle qui s'ensuivit ne pourrait trouver d'analogie que dans une panique nocturne de transatlantique, une explosion de batterie de jazz, un carnaval de jugement dernier, lorsque d'un seul élan trente sonnettes comme des vrilles taraudèrent les fondations de l'hôtel, et avec la majesté d'une sonde touchant le fond de la fosse des Philippines descendit vers moi comme un rideau de fenêtre la barbe du patriarche de l'Adriatique.

Venice

On that beach where snow was scurrying with the light foliage of foam, in the five o'clock sun, I was at the gate of the Martinengo palace, ringing the bell. I was alone at the geometric center of this colossal eyebrow of sand—a few minutes more and the blond squads of dunes sounding the retreat would block my way across the waves. Like a Bastille Day of fireworks and flags, the ringing permeated the drowsy corridors like oil, the bronze galleries of derisory, worthless armor, and disturbed the treasure chest beneath a shadow's fold. The pinewoods, in the background, suddenly looked like the mineral glow of spotlights when an orchestra plays the prelude to the clair de lune of *Werther*. I could say to myself, overjoyed, that this was solitude. Above me, solemn as a stage flat, the shutter of a high window was slamming in the wind amidst a galloping gust of sand. The thunderous sea, from one end of the bay to the other, shortened the way out of a dubious escape. With my left hand I was attempting to shatter, as delicately as possible, the glass of one of those charming eighteenth-century cases in which the mouth of a fire alarm is sometimes hidden. The ensuing spectacle might find its analogue only in the nighttime panic of a transatlantic ocean liner, an explosion of jazz drums, a carnival of the last judgment, when in a single burst thirty bells threaded like screws through the hotel's foundations, and with the grandiosity of a probe touching the bottom of the Philippine Trench, descending toward me like the curtain of a window, came the beard of the patriarch of the Adriatic Sea.

Transbaïkalie

Les rendez-vous manqués d'amoureux au creux d'une carrière
de porphyre — la géhenne et la gigue démente des bateaux en
feu, par une nuit de brume, sur la mer du Nord — les géantes
broussailles de ronces et les hautes couronnes de cimetière
d'une usine bombardée — ne pourraient donner qu'une faible
idée de ce vide pailleté de brûlures, de ce vau-l'eau et de cette
dérive d'épaves comme les hautes eaux de l'Amazone où mon
esprit n'avait cessé de flotter après le départ, au milieu d'énig-
matiques monosyllabes, de celle que je ne savais plus nommer
que par des noms de glaciers inaccessibles ou de quelques-unes
de ces splendides rivières mongoles aux roseaux chanteurs,
aux tigres blancs et odorants, à la tendresse d'oasis inutiles au
milieu des cailloutis brûlés des steppes, ces rivières qui défilent
si doucement devant le chant d'un oiseau perdu à la cime d'un
roseau, comme posé après un retrait du déluge sur un paysage
balayé des dernières touches de l'homme : Nonni, Kéroulèn,
Sélenga. Nonni, c'est le nom que je lui donne dans ses consola-
tions douces, ses grandes échappées de tendresse comme sous
des voiles de couvent, c'est la douceur de caillou de ses mains
sèches, sa petite sueur d'enfant, légère comme une rosée, après
l'étreinte matinale, c'est la petite sœur des nuits innocentes
comme des lis, la petite fille des jeux sages, des oreillers blancs
comme un matin frais de septembre — Kéroulèn ce sont
les orages rouges de ses muscles vaincus dans la fièvre, c'est
sa bouche tordue de cette éclatante torsion sculpturale des
poutrelles de fer après l'incendie, les grandes vagues vertes où
flottent ses jambes houleuses entre les muscles frais de la mer
quand je sombre avec elle comme une planche à travers des
strates translucides et ce grand bruit de cloches secouées qui

Transbaikalia

Missed encounters of lovers in the hollow of a porphyry
quarry—Gehenna and the demented dance of flaming boats,
on a foggy night, in the North Sea—giant bramble bushes and
a bombed factory's high cemetery wreaths—could give but
a faint idea of this void spangled with burns, of this drift of
debris and this stream flowing like the Amazon's high waters
where my mind had continued to float after the departure,
amid cryptic monosyllables, of the woman I could call only
by the names of inaccessible glaciers or a few of those splen-
did Mongolian rivers with singing reeds, with fragrant white
tigers, and the tenderness of useless oases amid the steppes'
scorched gravel, those rivers that unfurl so softly before the
song of a lost bird perched on the tip of a reed, as though
a flood had withdrawn after sweeping a landscape of man's
last traces: Nonni, Kherlen, Selenga. Nonni is the name I give
her when she softly consoles me, hushed and tender as if be-
hind a convent veil, it's the stony softness of her dry hands,
her little beads of sweat like a child's, light as a drop of dew
after morning's embrace, it's the little sister of nights pure as
lilies, the little girl of innocent games, of white pillows crisp
as a September morning—Kherlen is the red storms of her
muscles overcome in a fever, it's her mouth twisted by that
blazing sculptural torque of iron beams after a fire, the great
green waves where her jostling legs float among the sea's fresh
muscles when like a plank I sink with her through translucent
strata and the blare of trembling bells that follows us to the bed
of the depths—Selenga is when her dress floats like a sunlit
flock of seagulls amid the morning's empty streets, it's in large
fluttering veils, ocellated with her eyes like a peacock's tail, it's

nous accompagne sur la couche des profondeurs — Sélenga, c'est quand flotte sa robe comme un vol de mouettes ensoleillé au milieu des rues vides du matin, c'est dans de grands voiles battants, ocellés de ses yeux comme une queue d'oiseau à traîne, ce sont ses yeux liquides qui nagent autour d'elle comme une danse d'étoiles — c'est quand elle descend dans mes rêves par les cheminées calmes de décembre, s'assied près de mon lit et prend timidement ma main entre ses petits doigts pour le difficile passage à travers les paysages solennels de la nuit, et ses yeux transparents à toutes les comètes ouverts au-dessus de mes yeux jusqu'au matin.

her liquid eyes that swim around her like dancing stars—it's when she descends into my dreams through December's calm chimneys, sits near my bed, and timidly takes my hand between her small fingers for the difficult trip across the night's solemn landscapes, her eyes transparent to all the comets in the sky, open above my eyes till morning.

Le Vent froid de la nuit

Je l'attendais le soir dans le pavillon de chasse, près de la Rivière Morte. Les sapins dans le vent hasardeux de la nuit secouaient des froissements de suaire et des craquements d'incendie. La nuit noire était doublée de gel, comme le satin blanc sous un habit de soirée — au-dehors, des mains frisées couraient de toutes parts sur la neige. Les murs étaient de grands rideaux sombres, et sur les steppes de neige des nappes blanches, à perte de vue, comme des feux se décollent des étangs gelés, se levait la lumière mystique des bougies. J'étais le roi d'un peuple de forêts bleues, comme un pèlerinage avec ses bannières se range immobile sur les bords d'un lac de glace. Au plafond de la caverne bougeait par instants, immobile comme la moire d'une étoffe, le cyclone des pensées noires. En habit de soirée, accoudé à la cheminée et maniant un revolver dans un geste de théâtre, j'interrogeais par désœuvrement l'eau verte et dormante de ces glaces très anciennes ; une rafale plus forte parfois l'embuait d'une sueur fine comme celle des carafes, mais j'émergeais de nouveau, spectral et fixe, comme un marié sur la plaque du photographe qui se dégage des remous de plantes vertes. Ah ! les heures creuses de la nuit, pareilles à un qui voyage sur les os légers et pneumatiques d'un rapide — mais soudain elle était là, assise toute droite dans ses longues étoffes blanches.

The Cold Wind of the Night

I was waiting for her that evening at the hunting lodge, near the Morte River. The firs in the chaotic wind of the night trembled like shrouds rustling and fire crackling. The black night was lined with frost, a white satin slip under an evening dress—outside, wrinkled hands ran all over the snow. The walls were large dark curtains, and on the snowy steppes of the white tablecloths, as far as the eye could see, like fire ascending from the ice of frozen ponds, the mystical candlelight arose. I was the king of a people of blue forests, like a procession lining up with its banners, immobile on the banks of an icy lake. On the cave's ceiling, the cyclone of black thoughts, immobile as a fabric's shimmer, shifted now and then. In evening wear, my elbow propped on the mantelpiece, I wielded a revolver with a theatrical flourish and, with nothing better to do, examined the green, dormant water on those ancient mirrors; a stronger gust sometimes misted over the surface with a fine film of dew like condensation on a carafe, but I was emerging again, spectral and fixed in place, like a groom freeing himself from the swirls of green plants on a photographic plate. Ah! The hollow hours of the night, speeding by like a passenger on an express train's light, airy bones—but suddenly there she was, sitting up straight in her long white folds of fabric.

Pleine eau

Le cri d'un coq traîne par les rues vides, dans cette chaude après-midi de juin où il n'y a personne. Le silence, profond comme un grenier à blé abandonné, gorgé de chaleur et de poussière. Quel désœuvrement sous les voûtes basses de ces tilleuls, sur ces marteaux de portes où bâillent mille gueules de bronze ! Quel après-midi de dimanche *distingué*, qui fait rêver de gants noirs à crispins de dentelles aux bras des jeunes filles, d'ombrelles sages, de parfums inoffensifs, des steppes arides du cinq à sept ! Seul un petit nuage, alerte, blanc, — comme le nageur éclatant porté sur l'écume ombre soudain de stupidité la foule plantée sur la plage — couvre de confusion tout à coup le paysage endormi et fait rêver d'extravagance au fond de l'avenue un arbre qui n'a jamais encore volé.

Open Water

A cock's crow hangs in the empty streets, where no one's around on this hot June afternoon. Silence, deep as an abandoned granary, saturated with heat and dust. What idleness beneath the low vaults of these lime trees, on these door knockers where a thousand bronze mouths yawn! What a *distinguished* Sunday afternoon, bringing dreams of lacy black gloves on young girls' wrists, of poised parasols, of inoffensive scents, of arid steppes in the lull from five to seven! Only a small cloud, brisk and white—like a glimmering swimmer, carried by the foam, who suddenly casts a shadow of stupor over the crowd planted on the beach—abruptly showers confusion over the sleeping landscape and brings extravagant dreams at the way's end to a tree that has yet to fly.

Gang

Il y avait, toujours chargé au plein cœur de la ville, ce quartier tournant projetant par saccades vers les routes de banlieue le flot de ses voitures comme le barillet d'un revolver. C'est de là que nous partions pour les voyages-surprise et les soirs bordés d'églantines, les beaux matins des documentaires de pêche à la truite qui brassent à poignées tout un saladier de pierreries. Les doigts serrés sur le bordage de tôle, et le fleuve d'air sculptant un bec d'aigle et la majesté d'une figure de proue sous le casque de toile blanche. Au bout des robes blanches sur chaque boulevard d'huile noire, une forêt qui s'ouvre en coup de vent comme la mer Rouge — à l'enfilade de chaque flaque solaire, le lingot de glace que tronçonnent les massifs d'arbres — au bout de chaque branche, une fleur qui se déplie dans un claquement de linge — au bout de chaque bras, la rose brûlante d'un revolver.

Gang

There used to be, always loaded at the city's heart, that spinning neighborhood erratically projecting the flow of its cars toward the outlying roads, like a revolver's cylinder. From there we'd leave for spontaneous trips and evenings lined with sweetbriars, on clear mornings of trout-fishing documentaries that gather an entire bowl of precious stones. Fingers tight over a boat's metal frame, the river of air sculpting an eagle's beak, and the majesty of a figurehead under a white-canvas helmet. At the end of white dresses on each black-oil boulevard, a forest opening in a whirl like the Red Sea—along each puddle of light, the crystal ingot cut by clusters of trees—at the end of each branch, a flower unfolding in the whip of a cloth—at the end of each arm, the burning rose of a revolver.

Grand hôtel

Je suis d'une race tapageuse qui préfère à toute chose les après-midis affairés d'une ville de grand luxe, avant un gala d'opéra solennisant la plus longue pente de la journée, les après-midis torrides où le soleil bourdonne derrière les futaies épaisses des stores déployés sur la façade de l'hôtel comme une fête nautique, un pavoisement blanc et orgueilleux de régates au-dessus de l'huile noire de l'asphalte où le reflet tout mangé de flaques des feuillages se fait grêle irréellement. Je ne saurais sans dommage faire grâce au luxe d'aucun de ces détails de mauvais goût qui mystérieusement le poétisent : fourrures estivales, cascades mélancoliques des pourboires sonnant au long des escaliers de pierres tombales, fumoirs aux voix empanachées assommées par les cuirs de Cordoue, bars-nickels de garde-malades d'où l'horizon fuit vers les jetées — mais le luxe c'est surtout, pelotonné au fond de la voiture dans les coussins au cœur d'une soirée chaude, d'un horizon merveilleusement vert et dilaté de musiques proches, la face renversée contre le ciel vert comme des prairies, tout uni le long du visage le vent délicieux de la vitesse coûteuse, comme la belle simplicité retrouvée, la largesse princière, le dénuement antique de l'or pur coulant entre les doigts.

Grand Hotel

I belong to a boisterous race that likes more than anything the busy afternoons of a luxurious city, before an opera gala solemnizing the downward slope of day, those torrid afternoons when the sun hums behind dense thickets of awnings stretched over the hotel's facade, like a maritime festival's white flags proudly hoisted for a regatta, above the asphalt's black oil where the reflection of puddles eaten away by foliage thins out in illusion. I'd be doing a disservice to luxury by sparing it those tasteless details that mysteriously poeticize it: summer furs, melancholy cascades of change ringing along staircases of gravestones, smoking parlors with plumed voices dazed by cordovan leathers, nickel bars of railings from which the horizon flees toward the piers—but the sure mark of luxury is to be nestled in the back of a car amid cushions on a warm evening, with a marvelously green horizon swelling up with nearby strains of music, one's head cast upward against the meadow-green skies, one's face smoothed by the delicious wind at an extravagant speed, like beautiful simplicity regained, the princely largesse, the ancient deprivation of pure gold trickling between one's fingers.

Written in water

Certes, il me dure d'être condamné à cette malédiction de l'épaisseur. Ce corps comme une outre plombée, pourrissant comme tout ce qui a ventre, et toute la servitude humaine dans ce mot, mot qui décapite les étoiles, le plus dérisoire, le plus clownesque que recèle le langage, *graviter*. Rien ne m'a jamais bouleversé comme l'avatar souriant de promesse au pied de mon lit dans son cadre de peluche d'un personnage devenu miroir, — et, sans doute à la fin lourd d'un secret de divine paresse, dissous dans le plan et confié au médiateur le plus consolant qui soit pour moi de l'infini. Pourrait-on jamais vivre qu'à *fleur de peau*, se prendre à d'autres pièges qu'à ceux des glaces et — déplié comme ces belles peaux de bœuf qui boivent le ciel de toute leur longueur — déplissé, lissé comme une cire vierge au seuil des grands signes nocturnes — bouquet séché qui livre ses souvenirs dans le noir — devant cette photographie jaunie dans son cadre de peluche ai-je jamais pu me glisser, tarot mêlé au jeu du rêve, entre les feuillets de mon lit sans songer au jour où — sans âge comme un roi de cartes — familier comme le double gracieux des bas-reliefs d'Égypte — plat comme l'aïeul sur fond de mine de plomb, à la belle chemise de guillotiné, des albums de famille — désossé comme ces beaux morts des voitures de course dont le cœur se brise de se réveiller trop vite au creux d'un rêve splendide de lévitation — je retournerai hanter ma parfaite image.

Written in Water

It is, indeed, taxing to be condemned to this curse of thick-
ness. This body like a leaden sack, rotting like anything with
a stomach, and all of human bondage in this word, a word
that decapitates stars, the most derisive and humiliating word
that language contains: *gravitate.* Nothing has moved me more
than the promising reincarnation, smiling in a velvet frame
at the foot of my bed, of a figure that has become a mirror
image—as if, heavy with some secret of divine idleness, it had
dissolved in the glass, entrusting itself to the infinite's most
consoling mediator. Would it ever be possible to live *skin-deep,*
to be caught in traps other than mirrors and—stretched out
like those fine ox-hides whose entire length drinks in the sky—
smoothed over and spread out like virgin wax at the threshold
of grand nocturnal signs—a dried bouquet releasing its mem-
ories into the dark—before that yellowing photograph in its
velvet frame, have I ever managed to slip, tarot cards mixed
with the play of dreams, between the sheets of my bed with-
out thinking of the day when—ageless as a king of cards—
familiar as elegant copies of Egyptian bas-reliefs—dull as an
ancestor, in the fine shirt of a guillotined man, against the
graphite backdrop of family albums—weightless as the corpse
of a racecar whose bones shatter from waking too fast amid a
splendid dream of levitation—I'll return to haunt my perfect
image.

Le Jardin engourdi

Quelle tranquillité maintenant que midi sonné fait glisser la journée insensiblement sur sa pente la plus tragique. Les poiriers compliqués, branchus et durs comme des coraux, les asters, les mille feuilles, les herbes de la Saint-Jean poussent au travers des semis de coquilles d'huîtres, et les beaux galets font des chemins de plaisir, des routes douces entre les pelouses comme le contournement d'un sein. Par derrière le mur de mousses, la mer, debout à quarante-cinq degrés comme dans une chute d'automobile, grise comme la belle tonalité de la planète vue de Sirius, vraiment reposante — la mer fondamentale, à la fois juge et partie.

The Numbed Garden

Now that noon has struck, making the day slip seamlessly into its most tragic decline, how tranquil it is. The pear trees, intricate with their many branches, stiff as coral, the asters, the yarrow, the St. John's wort sprout from sown oyster shells, and the fine pebbles make pleasant roads, sweet paths curving through the grass like the contours of a breast. Behind a wall of moss, the sea, standing at 45 degrees like a falling automobile, gray as the lovely tonality of the planet seen from Sirius, truly calming—the fundamental sea, a judge in her own cause.

Isabelle Elisabeth

La singularité du visage d'*Isabelle* était faite de ces blancheurs de linge, de ces éclatantes étendues de mer calme entre deux coups de ressac, de ces plages accueillantes de lumière lisse d'un après-midi de juillet sur un toit d'ardoises. Une encolure choisie, faite pour les nobles harnais du cheval de bataille, ses seins plantés comme des chevilles pour l'escalade d'un bel arbre, la prise qu'ils appelaient de deux mains ouvertes et accueillantes, des yeux compliqués et préhensiles comme la vrille du pois de senteur, des volontés brutales et folâtres comme un coup de mer contre une jetée par le jour du plus beau temps, je me rappelle tout comme si c'était hier. Par-dessus toute qualité, j'admirais qu'elle pût être à ce point ambiguë — ses mains changent comme le vent, ses pieds lisses se posent par le monde sur je ne sais quel sonore ouragan de tuiles, et, singulière comme ces transmutations à vue qu'un prince charmant d'un haussement de sourcil encourage dans les enlacements de la Belle et de la Bête, c'est tout à coup d'un *profil perdu* de cette figure étrange sur un fond de forêts et de feuilles changeantes qu'est faite — maniaque et toujours à je ne sais quel souvenir perdu attentive — la beauté du visage d'Élisabeth.

Isabelle Elisabeth

The singularity of *Isabelle*'s face was made up of those linen whites, those dazzling stretches of calm sea between backwash waves, those welcoming beaches of a July afternoon's smooth light on a slate roof. A fine neck, shaped for a battle horse's noble harness, her breasts firm as pegs for climbing a lovely tree, beckoning the hold of two welcoming and open hands, eyes complicated and prehensile as a sweet pea's tendrils, desires violent and wild as a sea crashing against a pier on the loveliest of days—I remember everything as if it were yesterday. More than any other quality, I admired that she could be so ambiguous—her hands changing like the wind, her smooth feet landing on some resounding hurricane of tiles, and, singular as those visual transformations that a prince charming, raising an eyebrow, encourages in the embraces of Beauty and the Beast, suddenly in that strange figure's *profil perdu*, against a backdrop of forests and changing leaves, there took shape—maniacal and attentive to some lost memory—the beauty of *Elisabeth*'s face.

La Barrière de Ross

Il faut se lever matin pour voir le jour monter à l'horizon de la banquise, à l'heure où le soleil des latitudes australes étale au loin des chemins sur la mer. Miss Jane portait son ombrelle, et moi un élégant fusil à deux coups. À chaque défilé de glacier, nous nous embrassions dans les crevasses de menthe, et retardions à plaisir le moment de voir le soleil à boulets rouges s'ouvrir un chemin dans un chantilly de glace pailletée. Nous longions de préférence le bord de la mer là où, la falaise respirant régulièrement avec la marée, son doux roulis de pachyderme nous prédisposait à l'amour. Les vagues battaient sur les murs de glace des neiges bleues et vertes, et jetaient à nos pieds dans les anses des fleurs géantes de cristaux, mais l'approche du jour était surtout sensible à ce léger ourlet de phosphore qui courait sur les festons de leur crête, comme quand les capitales nocturnes se prennent à voguer sur l'étale de leur haute mer. Au Cap de la Dévastation, dans les fissures de la glace poussaient des edelweiss couleur de nuit bleue, et nous étions toujours sûrs de voir se renouveler de jour en jour une provision fraîche de ces œufs d'oiseaux de mer dont Jane pensait qu'ils ont la vertu d'éclaircir le teint. Sur la bouche de Jane, c'était un rite pour moi que de renouveler chaque jour pour l'y cueillir de mes lèvres cet adage puéril. Parfois les nuages nous dérobant le pied de la falaise annonçaient un ciel couvert pour l'après-midi, et Jane s'informait d'une voix menue si j'avais soigneusement enveloppé les sandwiches au chester. Enfin la falaise devenait plus haute et toute crayeuse de soleil, c'était la Pointe de la Désolation, et sur un signe de Jane j'étendais la couverture sur la neige fraîche. Nous demeurions là longtemps couchés, à écouter battre du poitrail les chevaux sauvages de

Ross Ice Shelf

One must rise early to see the day ascend over the ice floe's horizon, at the hour when the sun of the southern latitudes spreads paths onto the sea in the distance. Miss Jane carried her parasol, I an elegant double-barreled shotgun. At every glacier gorge, we'd kiss in the mint crevasses and take pleasure in lingering to see the fiery sun carve a path through a lacework of glittering ice. We liked to walk along the shore where, the cliff breathing steadily with the tide, the sea's soft, thick rolling predisposed us to love. The waves beat against the walls of blue and green snow, and threw giant crystal flowers at our feet in the coves, but the day's approach was especially perceptible on that faint hem of phosphorus that lined the scallops of the waves' crests, as when capital cities set sail at night on the stillness of high seas. At the Cape of Devastation, in the fissures of ice, grew edelweiss the color of midnight blue, and we were always sure to see, day after day, a fresh supply of those seabird eggs that Jane believed could brighten one's complexion. It was a daily rite for me to repeat Jane's words on her mouth, as if to gather them with my lips. Sometimes the clouds concealing the cliff's foot announced an overcast sky for the afternoon, and Jane asked in a small voice whether I'd taken care to wrap the Cheshire cheese sandwiches. Eventually the cliff grew higher and chalky from the sun: that was Desolation Peak, and on Jane's signal I spread the blanket over the fresh snow. We lay there a long while, listening to the sea's wild horses beating their chests in the icy caves. The horizon of the open sea was a diamond blue semicircle submerging a wall of ice, where sometimes a flake of vapor emerged, protruding from the sea like a white

la mer dans les cavernes de glace. L'horizon du large était un demi-cercle d'un bleu diamanté que sous-tendait le mur de glace, où parfois un flocon de vapeur naissait, décollé de la mer comme une voile blanche — et Jane me citait les vers de Lermontov. J'aurais passé là des après-midis entières, la main dans les siennes, à suivre le croassement des oiseaux de mer, et à lancer des morceaux de glace que nous écoutions tomber dans le gouffre, pendant que Jane comptait les secondes, la langue un peu tirée d'application comme une écolière. Alors nous nous étreignions si longtemps et de si près que dans la neige fondue se creusait une seule rigole plus étroite qu'un berceau d'enfant, et, quand nous nous relevions, la couverture entre les mamelons blancs faisait songer à ces mulets d'Asie qui descendent des montagnes bâtées de neige.

Puis le bleu de la mer s'approfondissait et la falaise devenait violette ; c'était l'heure où le froid brusque du soir détache de la banquise ces burgs de cristal qui croulent dans une poussière de glace avec le bruit de l'éclatement d'un monde, et retournent sous la volute cyclopéenne d'une vague bleue un ventre de paquebot gercé d'algues sombres, ou ébrouement lourd d'un bain de plésiosaures. Pour nous seuls s'allumait de proche en proche, jusqu'au bord de l'horizon, cette canonnade de fin de monde comme un Waterloo des solitudes — et longtemps encore la nuit tombée, très froide, était trouée dans le grand silence du jaillissement lointain de fantômes des hauts geysers de plumes blanches — mais j'avais déjà serré dans les miennes la main glacée de Jane, et nous revenions à la lumière des pures étoiles antarctiques.

sail—and Jane recited Lermontov to me. I could have spent entire afternoons there, my hand in hers, following the cawing of seabirds, and tossing chunks of ice into the chasm and listening to them fall, while Jane counted the seconds, sticking out her tongue in concentration like a schoolgirl. Then we embraced each other for so long and so tightly that a single channel narrower than a baby's cradle formed in the melted snow, and when we got back up, the blanket among the white knolls brought to mind those Asian mules that descend from mountains laden with snow.

Then the sea's blue deepened and the cliff turned purple; it was the hour when the evening's sudden cold detaches from the ice floe those crystal castles that crumble into a dust of ice with the sound of a bursting world, turning over, under a blue wave's gigantic scroll, the belly of a liner with dark algae in its cracks, or the heavy snorting of swimming plesiosaurs. For us alone there grew brighter and brighter, up to the edge of the horizon, that apocalyptic cannonade like a Waterloo of solitudes—and, for a long time, the freezing night, in the great silence, was punctured by distant ghosts gushing forth from tall, white-feather geysers—but I had already squeezed Jane's icy hand in mine, and we were coming back to the light of pure Antarctic stars.

L'Averse

Voici le monde couvé sous la pluie, la chaleur moite, le toit des gouttes et des brindilles, et les molles couvertures d'air aux mille piqûres d'éclaboussements. Voici la belle sur son lit d'eau, toute éveillée par la soudaine transparence fraîche, toute coïncidante à une pure idée d'elle-même, toute dessinée comme l'eau par le verre. Dans l'air où nagent les balbutiantes étoiles de l'eau, une main d'air sort de l'alcôve verdissante aux parfums d'herbe et suspend à l'embrasse de lianes les courtines emperlées et l'arithmétique crépitante du boulier de cristal.

Rainfall

Here is the world cocooned beneath rain, the moist warmth, the roof of droplets and twigs, the soft blankets of air with a thousand splashing stings. Here is beauty on her bed of water, awakened by the sudden fresh transparency, attuned to a pure idea of herself, drawn like water by glass. In the air where the water's babbling stars swim, a hand of air emerges from the greening alcove fragrant with grass, and suspends from the tieback of lianas pearl-studded canopies and the crackling arithmetic of a crystal abacus.

Vergiss mein nicht

Ce que tu fais à cette heure tardive de la nuit ? Peut-être assise à coudre dans cette lumière bonne des soirées diligentes, des mains soigneuses, cette foisonnante envie du bon ouvrage qui délie les langues pour un babil bienveillant sous la lampe, et les chaudes pensées gaies qu'on distribue à la ronde à l'absent amical — peut-être à la fenêtre devant un bois de pins sous la lune brillante, tu touches le grand froid minéral qui rôde entre les planètes avec les doigts mouillés de ta main, et tu penses que je suis loin, derrière cet horizon où s'enfonce un train empenné de ses douces lumières, si enivré de son bruit de fer dans la nuit calme — peut-être un livre me trahit-il dans un battement d'éventail de ces pages tournées dans la fièvre au vent doux d'une chevelure, et des infortunes te bouleversent où rien ne te paraîtrait tout à coup plus malséant que j'aie aucune part — ou bien dans la chambre où tu t'endors, où soudain tout me déserte et t'oriente selon les mystérieux indices du prochain matin, tu coules au milieu de tes rêves dans l'enivrement d'être si seule, et travaille avec délices pour les voleurs de nuit toute une ruche de mauvaises abeilles.

Vergiss Mein Nicht

What is it you're doing this late at night? Sewing, perhaps, in the good light of diligent evenings, with deft hands, this bubbling desire for good work that loosens tongues for a benevolent babble under the lamp, and the warm, bright thoughts given to the friend who's away—perhaps at the window, before a pine forest under the shining moon, your damp fingers touch the great mineral cold that roams among planets, and you think I'm far away, behind the horizon where a train sinks, with its sweet, feathery light, so drunk on its iron noise in the calm night—perhaps a book betrays me in a fanning of these pages turned passionately in the gentle wind of hair, and you're unsettled by misfortunes that suddenly appear more unseemly to you than if I were involved—or perhaps in the bedroom where you fall asleep, where everything suddenly deserts me and guides you according to the morning's mysterious hints, you glide through your dreams, drunk on being so alone, and take pleasure in making a vicious beehive for the thieves of the night.

Inabordable

C'est une femme jeune sous les pas de laquelle les images se lèvent à foison. Parfois, dans un sentier d'avril, elle dresse une main molle et douce comme de la plume et calme comme à regret les inquiétudes du paysage — ou bien le paraphe mystérieux de sa démarche entre des marges de bitume le dispute au plus bel instrument du littérateur. J'aime à suivre dans les méandres d'une rue colorée le fil de cette mélodie de mort subite que son apparition répercute d'un bord à l'autre de l'horizon de façades. Quelle rue sonore — d'un saccage de théâtre, de devantures brisées, de crieurs de journaux hurlant le plus bel assassinat du siècle, quelle verroterie colorée de sang, quel beau sang écumeux et chantant comme des trilles, comme des arpèges, quelle molle inflexion de saxophone vaudra jamais pour moi le regard qu'elle verse du coin de son œil précis et calme, le ruisseau magnétique de son regard qui coule à pleins bords entre les maisons comme la salive acide d'un glacier ?

Unattainable

She's a young woman beneath whose steps images arise in profusion. Sometimes, on an April path, she raises a hand, soft and light as a plume, and slowly calms the landscape's disquiet—or else her gait's mysterious print between asphalt margins rivals the finest instrument of a *littérateur*. Along the meanderings of a colorful street, I like to follow that melodious thread of sudden death which her appearance echoes back and forth on the horizon of facades. No ringing street—with a ransacked theater, shattered storefronts, town criers announcing the century's finest assassination, no glassware stained with blood, no fine foaming blood singing like trills, like arpeggios, no saxophone's soft inflection will ever, for me, compare to the gaze she sheds from the corner of her eye, calm and sharp, her gaze's magnetic stream flowing along the banks, between the houses, like the acidic saliva of a glacier.

Villes hanséatiques

Éveil d'une jeune beauté couchée sur le gazon près d'une ville, devant l'étincellement de l'eau et la paresse de dix heures, sous la lumière bleuâtre. Les clochetons et les tours de cette ville très ancienne, ses hautes rues étroites pour le grondement et les émeutes de la foule affamée des sièges, les arbres somptueux du mail pour ombrager les bijoux trop riches, éteindre les velours orgueilleux et fermer une résille de soleil sur les cheveux des jeunes femmes aux jours de triomphe et de parade, et les places triangulaires sous le soleil cruel avec leurs senteurs puissantes d'immondices. L'air coule et lave les ponts comme un fleuve bleu en spirales musicales. La petite ville noble dentelle un abrupt de rêve sur l'horizon au-delà d'une prairie de fête coupée par un fleuve, mais toute la lumière chaude est pour approfondir sur le foin coupé l'arôme d'une chevelure étouffante, et ourler un pied et une main nue dont les doigts jouent sur les cordes compliquées de l'air.

Hanseatic Cities

Awakening of a young beauty lying on the grass near a city, before the sparkling water and the idleness of ten o'clock, under the bluish light. The turrets and towers of this ancient city, its streets high and narrow for the rumble and riots of crowds hungry for sieges, the walkway lined with sumptuous trees to provide shade for opulent jewelry, to dull proud velvets and throw a net of sunlight over young women's hair on days of triumph and parades, the triangular squares stinking of filth under the cruel sun. The air flows and washes the bridges in musical spirals like a blue river. The small noble city serrates the horizon with a dreamlike precipice beyond a festive meadow crossed by a river, but all the warm light serves to intensify the scent of stifling hair on cut hay, and to outline a foot and a bare hand whose fingers play on the intricate strings of the air.

Salon meublé

Dans le jour très sombre — de cette nuance spécialement
sinistre que laissent filtrer par un après-midi d'août torride
les persiennes rabattues sur une chambre mortuaire — sur les
murs peints de cet enduit translucide, visqueux pour l'œil et
au toucher dur comme le verre, qui tapisse les cavernes à sta-
lactites, une légère écharpe d'eau sans bruit, comme sur les
ardoises des vespasiennes, frissonnante, moirée, douce comme
de la soie. Les rigoles confluant dans un demi-jour à l'angle
gauche de la pièce nourrissent avant de s'échapper une minus-
cule cressonnière. Côté droit, dans une grande cage de Faraday
à l'épreuve des coups de foudre, jetée négligemment sur le
bras d'une chaise curule comme au retour d'une promenade
matinale, la toge ensanglantée de César, reconnaissable à son
étiquette de musée et l'aspect *sui generis* de déchirures partic-
ulièrement authentiques. Une horloge suisse rustique, à deux
tons, avec caille et coucou, sonnant les demies et les quarts
pour le silence d'aquarium. Sur la cheminée, victimes de je
ne sais quelle spécialement préméditée mise en évidence au
milieu d'une profusion de bibelots *beaucoup* plus somptueux,
un paquet de scaferlati entamé et la photographie en premier
communiant (carton fort, angles abattus, tranche épaisse et
dorée, travail sérieux pour familles catholiques, avec la sig-
nature du photographe) du président Sadi-Carnot. Dans la
pénombre du fond du salon, un wagon de marchandises avec
son échauguette, sur sa voie de garage légèrement persillée de
pâquerettes et d'ombellifères, laisse suinter par sa porte entre-
bâillée l'étincellement d'un service en porcelaine de Sèvres, et
le bel arrangement des petits verres à liqueur.

Furnished Parlor

In the dark light—an especially ominous gloom, the kind that, on a sweltering August afternoon, passes through shutters closed over a morgue—on the walls coated with this translucent glaze, which covers stalactite caves, viscous to the eye and hard to the touch like glass, a light scarf of water silently fluttering, as on the slate stalls of *vespasiennes*, shimmering, soft as silk. The channels flowing together amid a semi-darkness in the room's back left corner feed into a miniature watercress pond before slipping away. On the right, in a large Faraday cage immune to lightning strikes, tossed carelessly onto the armrests of a curule chair as though after a morning walk, Caesar's bloody toga, identifiable by its museum label and the *sui generis* look of particularly authentic rips. A rustic Swiss clock, two-toned with quails and cuckoos, sounding the half and quarter hours for an aquarium silence. On the mantelpiece, victims of some expressly prearranged display amid a *much* more sumptuous wealth of trinkets, an opened pack of Scaferlati, and a photograph of President Sadi-Carnot's first Communion (sturdy cardstock, faded corners, thick and gilded border, serious craftsmanship for Catholic families, with the photographer's signature). In the penumbra at the back of the parlor, a freight car with its bartizan, on its siding sprinkled lightly with daisies and umbellifers, lets seep through its half-open door the scintillating set of Sèvres china, and the fine arrangement of small liqueur glasses.

Un hibernant

Le matin en s'éveillant, les doubles fenêtres l'emprisonnaient dans la forêt vierge de leur délicate palmeraie de glace. Il n'était besoin que de les arroser pour qu'elle poussât en une nuit. On s'étonnait cependant à peine de marcher la tête en bas : le ciel n'était plus que du terreau gris sale, mais la voie lactée de la neige éclairait le monde par-dessous. Tous les visages étaient beaux, rajeunis, — la neige enfantait des corps glorieux. À midi dans le jardin de neige et d'ouate, debout sur un pied et retenant son souffle, il réaccordait le silence. Le soir le labyrinthe duveteux du brouillard cadenassait la maison, — les portes restaient battantes. Puis le rayon de lune rôdait autour de la chambre jusqu'à ce que la fenêtre posât sur le lit une grande croix noire. Ces délicates escroqueries lumineuses pourtant n'étaient pas toujours sans danger.

A Hibernator

In the morning upon waking, the double windows imprisoned him in their virgin forest, a delicate palm grove of ice. It was only a question of watering those windows for the forest to grow in a single night. One would hardly be surprised, however, to find oneself walking upside down: the sky was nothing but gray dirty loam, though the milky way of snow lit the world below. Every face was beautiful, rejuvenated—the snow bore glorious bodies. At noon, in the garden of snow and cotton wool, standing on one foot and holding his breath, he retuned the silence. In the evening, the fleecy labyrinth of fog secured the house—the doors were left swinging. Then the moonbeam prowled around the room till the window set a large black cross on the bed. Such delicate, luminous ruses, however, weren't always without danger.

Les Nuits blanches

Comme la figure de proue d'un vaisseau à trois ponts four-
voyé dans ce port de galères, au-dessus de la Méditerranée plate
dont le blanc des vagues semble toujours fatigué d'un excès de
sel se levait pour moi derrière une correcte, une impeccable
rangée de verres à alcools, le visage de cette femme violente.
Derrière, c'était les grands pins mélancoliques, de ceux dont
l'orientation des branches ne laisse guère filtrer que les rayons
horizontaux du soleil à cette heure du couchant où les routes
sont belles, pures, livrées à la chanson des fontaines. On en-
tendait dans le fond du port des marteaux sur les coques, in-
finis, inlassables comme une chanson de toile au-dessus d'un
bâti naïf de tapisserie balayé de deux tresses blondes, circon-
venu d'un lacis incessant de soucis domestiques, avec au milieu
ces deux yeux doux, fatigués sous les boucles, la sœur même
des fontaines intarissables. On ne se fatiguait pas de boire, un
liquide clair comme une vitre, un alcool chantant et matinal.
Mais c'était à la fin un alanguissement de bon aloi, et tout à
coup comme si l'on avait dépassé l'heure *permise* — surpris le
port sous cette lumière défendue où descendent à l'improviste
pour un coup de main les beaux pirates des nuits septentrio-
nales, les lavandières bretonnes à la faveur d'un rideau de bru-
mes — c'était tout à coup le murmure des peupliers et la mor-
sure du froid humide — puis le claquement d'une portière et
c'était la sortie des théâtres dans le Petrograd des nuits blanches,
un arroi de fourrures inimaginable, l'opacité laiteuse et dure de
la Baltique — dans une aube salie de crachements rudes, pro-
longée des lustres irréels, la rue qui déverse une troïka sur les
falaises du large, un morne infini de houles grises comme une
fin du monde — c'était déjà l'heure d'aller aux Îles.

White Nights

Like the figurehead of a three-decker ship led astray into this port of galleys, above the calm Mediterranean Sea whose white waves always seem worn out by an excess of salt, there rose before me, behind a straight, impeccable row of liqueur glasses, the face of that violent woman. Behind her were large melancholy pines, the kind whose orientation of branches allows hardly anything to filter through except the horizontal rays at that sunset hour when roads are lovely, pure, and given to fountain songs. Deep in the port, hammers on the hulls could be heard, as infinite and indefatigable as a *chanson de toile* above the naive stitches of a needlepoint grazed by two blond braids and surrounded by an incessant lacis of domestic troubles, with those two soft eyes in the middle, tired under curls, the very sister of ever-flowing fountains. We never grew weary of imbibing, a liquid clear as glass, a melodious morning drink. But by day's end our languor was complete, and suddenly, as though we'd stayed *after* hours, we saw the port under that forbidden light, when strapping pirates of northern nights, Breton washerwomen thanks to a curtain of fog, unexpectedly come ashore in a surprise attack—suddenly there were whispering poplars and the biting damp cold—then a slamming door and people leaving theaters in the white nights of Petrograd, an unimaginable train of furs, the milky, hard opacity of the Baltic Sea—in a dawn stained with harsh spit, drawn out by illusory glows, the street releasing a troika onto the cliffs by the open sea, an infinity of gray swells, forlorn as the end of the world—it was already time to go to the Islands.

Robespierre

Cette beauté d'ange que l'on prête malgré soi — par-delà les
pages poussiéreuses d'un livre feuilleté jamais autrement que
dans la fièvre — , à quelques-uns des terroristes mineurs : Saint-
Just, Jacques Roux, Robespierre le Jeune — , cette beauté que
leur conserve pour nous à travers les siècles, nageant autour
d'une guirlande de gracieuses têtes coupées comme un baume
d'Égypte, le surnom de l'Incorruptible — ces blancheurs de
cous de Jean-Baptiste affilées par la guillotine, ces bouillons
de dentelles, ces gants blancs et ces culottes jaunes, ces bou-
quets d'épis, ces cantiques, ce déjeuner de soleil avant les
grandes cènes révolutionnaires, ces blondeurs de blé mûris-
sant, ces arcs flexibles des bouches engluées par un songe de
mort, ces roucoulements de Jean-Jacques sous la sombre ver-
dure des premiers marronniers de mai, verts comme jamais
du beau sang rouge des couperets, ces madrigaux funèbres
de Brummels somnambules, une botte de pervenches à la
main, ces affaissements de fleur, de vierges aristocrates dans
le panier à son — comme si, de savoir être un jour portées
seules au bout d'une pique, toute la beauté fascinante de la
nuit de l'homme eût dû affluer au visage magnétique de ces
têtes de Méduse — cette chasteté surhumaine, cette ascèse,
cette beauté sauvage de fleur coupée qui fait pâlir le visage de
toutes les femmes — c'est la langue de feu qui pour moi çà et
là descend mystérieusement au milieu des silhouettes rapides
comme des éclairs des grandes rues mouvantes comme sur
l'écran d'une allée d'arbres en flammes dans la campagne par
une nuit de juin, et me désigne à certaine extase panique le
visage inoubliable de quelques guillotinés de naissance.

Robespierre

That angelic beauty reluctantly ascribed—beyond the dusty
pages of a book one can leaf through only in a fever—to some
of the minor figures of the Reign of Terror: Saint-Just, Jacques
Roux, Robespierre the Younger—their beauty preserved for
us over the centuries, floating like an Egyptian balm around
a garland of elegant severed heads, by the nickname "the
Incorruptible"—those necks of Jean-Baptiste's, their whiteness
sharpened by the guillotine, those streams of lace, those white
gloves and those yellow culottes, those bundles of grain, those
canticles, that sunlit luncheon preceding grand revolutionary
suppers, that blondness of ripening wheat, those supple curves
of mouths set in place by the thought of death, Jean-Jacques's
coos beneath the dark verdure of the first chestnut trees to
bloom in May, their leaves shaded a peculiar green from the
fine red blood of the guillotine blades, those funereal mad-
rigals of sleepwalking dandies, a bouquet of periwinkles in
hand, those flowers and virgin aristocrats dropped into the
bran basket—as if, from knowing that one day they'd be led
to the end of a pike, all the enchanting beauty of the night
of man had flowed into the magnetic faces of those Medusan
heads—that superhuman chastity, that asceticism, that wild
beauty of picked flowers that makes every woman's face grow
pale—that is the language of fire which mysteriously descends
for me here and there amidst the lightning-quick silhouettes
of the shifting wide streets, as on the screen of flaming trees
in a country path on a June night, and reveals to me, in a cer-
tain panicked ecstasy, the unforgettable faces of some of the
guillotined by birth.

Les Affinités électives

Un grand palais aux corridors nuageux — par-devant des perspectives de soleil et de brumes, ce plain-chant matinal du soleil sur les bancs de brouillard qui se déchirent aux pointes des phares, un novembre perpétuel d'averses chantantes, d'oiseaux perdus qui d'un seul cri débarrassent le large — , par-derrière une pelouse domestique avec volière et vue de gazomètre — je me retirais là pour des semaines, pour des vacances libres, des parties de plaisir, de seul à seul multipliés comme un jeu de glaces, comme des perspectives en trompe-l'œil. Les méandres des corniches s'accommodaient de ce *jour* spécial des monuments battus par les marées. Le seul mobilier était de sextants, de sphères méridiennes, d'astrolabes faussés et en général tout ce qui peut jeter un doute pour une cervelle pensante sur la prévision accablante d'une suite de jours par trop conforme à l'index du calendrier. Par les jours de soleil trop cru, on étalait sur des espars une tapisserie de brumes, à l'aplomb architectural des moulures pendait à sécher la belle lessive des trois-mâts longs courriers, un luxe de batistes lourdes comme des brocarts, de vélums fantomatiques, et, gonflé, pansu, énorme comme l'armoire vernie de la coque d'où jaillissent les suaires géants du beau temps, le palais voguait sur un entre-deux de planètes, un éther fécondé de béantes mamelles blanches, de cumulus de toiles, d'un maelström claquant de blancheurs, l'impudeur géante d'un lâcher de voiles de mariée.

Elective Affinities

A grand palace with cloudy corridors—golden rays and mist
ahead, the sun's morning plainsong above blankets of fog bro-
ken by the tips of lighthouses, a perpetual November of sing-
ing showers, of lost birds clearing the open sea with a single
cry—behind it, a lawn with an aviary and a view of a gas-
ometer—I'd retire there for weeks, for leisurely vacations, in-
dulgent excursions, intimate conversations, endless as a game
of mirrors or an optical illusion. The winding coastal roads
yielded to that special *light* of tide-beaten monuments. The
only furnishings were sextants, meridian spheres, bent astro-
labes, and, in general, anything that might cast doubt on the
oppressive forecast for a course of days that conforms too well
to the seasonal signs. On days glaring with sunlight, a tapestry
of mist spread across the spars; above the moldings, the three-
masted windjammers' lovely laundered sails hung out to dry, a
host of ghostly velum clouds, batistes heavy as brocade; and—
bulging, hefty, enormous as the hull, a varnished wardrobe
from which the fine weather's giant shrouds spring forth—
the palace set sail between planets in an ether pregnant with
white teats, a cumulus of canvas, a flapping white maelstrom,
the great indecency of letting bridal veils fall.

Les Trompettes d'Aïda

De grands paysages secrets, intimes comme le rêve, sans cesse tournoyaient et se volatilisaient sur elle comme l'encens léger des nuages sur la flèche incandescente d'une cime. Sa venue était pareille à la face de lumière d'une forêt contemplée d'une tour, au soleil qu'exténuent les brouillards d'une côte pluvieuse, au chant fortifiant de la trompette sur les places agrandies du matin. Près d'elle j'ai rêvé parfois d'un cavalier barbare, au bonnet pointu, à califourchon sur son cheval nain comme sur une raide chaise d'église, tout seul et minuscule d'un trot de jouet mécanique à travers les steppes de la Mongolie — et d'autres fois c'était quelque vieil empereur bulgaroctone, pareil à une châsse parcheminée entrant dans Sainte-Sophie pour les actions de grâces, pendant que sous l'herbe des siècles sombre le pavé couleur d'os de Byzance et que l'orgasme surhumain des trompettes tétanise le soleil couchant.

The Trumpets of Aida

Grand secret landscapes, intimate as dreams, incessantly swirled and evaporated above her like the faint incense of clouds above a peak's glowing spire. Her arrival was like the bright side of a forest overlooked by a tower, like the sun dulled by a rainy coast's fog, like the trumpet's fortifying song in squares widened by the morning light. Near her, I've dreamt at times of a barbarian cavalier with a pointed cap, astride his pony as if on a stiff chapel chair, alone, tiny, trotting like a mechanical toy across the Mongolian steppes—other times it'd be some old Bulgar-Slayer emperor, like a parchment reliquary entering Hagia Sophia for thanksgivings; meanwhile, Byzantium's bone-colored cobbles sink under centuries-old grass and the trumpets' superhuman orgasm cripples the setting sun.

Unité originairement synthétique de l'aperception

Non, je ne suis pas venu pour cela, si c'est ce qui te tourmente. Laisse donc. À quoi bon ! — pas de gestes — nous nous entendons mieux que tu ne penses. C'était pendant que tu dormais à *poings fermés* que cette idée m'était venue. L'expression est curieuse — avoue-le — mais j'ai prise au besoin ailleurs que dans les défauts du langage, et je ne saurais lire à livre ouvert dans de si curieux épanchements nocturnes. Il n'y a rien là qui puisse te blesser.

Je me suis trouvé, puis perdu dans les couloirs de ce théâtre, comme une aiguille dans une botte de foin.

J'avais rencontré en rêve une femme fort belle. Tu ris déjà, tu crois ne pouvoir supporter une allégorie aussi bouffonne. Pourtant, je suis plus vieux que tu ne penses.

Une figure de style t'accompagnait quand tu croyais te porter seule à d'aussi coupables extrémités.

J'ai ce pouvoir. Mais une minute encore, et ce sera trop tard. La chance d'une porte entrebâillée sur une lumière, qui claque au moment où on passe devant, très tard, dans ces couloirs d'hôtel d'une ville inconnue où tout désoriente. Naturellement, on n'entre jamais.

J'ai eu le plaisir de saluer ce matin le poète Francis Jammes, au volant de son cylindre à vapeur.

Tu n'as pas de secrets pour moi. Les serrures que tu poses çà et là sur les portes douteuses par où tu t'évades ? Je suis revenu *aussi* des coups de tête et des portes qui claquent sur un circuit monotone, comme des salles de musée où tout ramène à l'issue du fatigant manège de chevaux de bois. Non, je voulais parler seulement de cette intonation singulière, *un peu* trop aiguë — tendue si tu veux — que tu prenais à ce week-end de

Original Synthetic Unity of Apperception

No, that's not why I came, if that's what's tormenting you. Never mind then. It's no use—stop gesticulating—we get along better than you think. It was while you were *fast* asleep that this idea came to me. The expression is curious—you must admit—but I have a hold, if need be, on areas other than language's defects, and I'm unable to sight-read in such curious outpourings of feeling at night. Nothing I've said can hurt you.

I found, then lost myself in the halls of this theater, like a needle in a haystack.

I'd met a beautiful woman in a dream. You're already laughing, you don't think you can stand such a silly allegory. But I'm older than you think.

A figure of speech accompanied you when you thought yourself alone in pursuing such shameful extremes.

I have that power. But one more minute, and it'll be too late. The possibility of a door opening onto a light, slamming at the moment one passes by, late at night, in the halls of an unknown city where everything is disorienting. Naturally, no one ever enters.

This morning I had the pleasure of greeting the poet Francis Jammes, at the wheel of his steam engine.

You don't keep any secrets from me. And the locks you put here and there on the shadowy doors where you slip away? I *too* have gotten over sudden impulses and doors slamming in a monotonous cycle, as in museum galleries where everything comes back to a tedious merry-go-round. No, I just wanted to talk about that singular, *slightly* sharp tone—tense, if you will—you used that weekend last June, when you told me about the time you traveled in an overcrowded train car.

juin dernier pour me raconter ton voyage dans un wagon excessivement comble. Longtemps, cette note un peu flûtée fit pour moi baisser d'un degré l'intensité du jour, si parfois je la retrouvais dans ces méandres d'une conversation à bâtons rompus où je l'avoue tu excelles. Des bêtises.

J'ai connu une maison où on servait les petits fours dans des feuilles de roses — mais tout de même, trop, c'est trop.

Ce sont de bien grands mots. Pourtant, en quittant Lucien à la sortie du théâtre, j'ai trouvé ta conduite singulière. La conversation, c'est vrai, s'était mal engagée ! Lucien est un charmant garçon. À tous points de vue. Mais tu es nerveuse.

J'ai deux grands bœufs dans mon étable. Cela peut surprendre — mais après tout n'a que la valeur d'une *simple constatation*.

J'ai pensé à Hélène, en lisant le dernier roman de Mauriac. Tu ne trouves pas ? Tous ces chagrins ont beaucoup abrégé la vie de sa mère.

Nous faisons un brin de causette dans les couloirs du métro, quand je descends vider mon seau de toilette.

Non, rien. C'était une idée. Tu vas rire. Mais, comme les adolescents vont dans les musées bien tenus rêver de préférence sur la solution d'un humble problème technique — moi je me suis souvent surpris à contempler une statue de Jeanne d'Arc, ou la photographie d'une pêcheuse de crevettes — , captivé toujours au-delà de toute mesure par l'image absorbante d'une femme prolongée par un étendard.

For a long time, that faintly dulcet tone slightly lowered the day's intensity for me, if at times I'd hear it in those meanderings of a conversation about this and that at which, I admit, you excel. Trifles.

I once knew of a place that served *petits fours* in rose leaves—but even so, enough is enough.

These are good big words. But on leaving Lucien outside the theater, I found your behavior peculiar. The conversation, it's true, had gotten off to a bad start! Lucien is a charming boy. In every respect. But you're nervous.

I have two large oxen in my stable. That might be surprising—but then again, everything is but a *simple observation*.

I thought about Hélène while reading Mauriac's last novel. Didn't you? All those sorrows cut short his mother's life.

We have a quick chat in the metro halls when I go down to empty my slop pail.

No, nothing. It was just an idea. You're going to laugh. But like teenagers who go into tidy museums, hoping to dream up the solution to a humble technical problem—I've often found myself contemplating a statue of Joan of Arc, or the photograph of a woman fishing for shrimp—always captivated beyond measure by the absorbing image of a woman extended by a standard.

Scandales mondains

Le jour se lève dans une pluie d'éclairs de chaleur, salué par de maternelles chutes de neige. Le travailleur à la chaîne, habile à scander de l'index le mol écoulement des minutes, soudain croit à une rémission particulière de son rêve, et s'endort. Les bielles et les courroies de transmission sont tout à coup jonchées de primevères. Le monde sommeille, le temps à peine d'éternuer un *Ave Maria*.

Ce canal sous la lumière éclatante de février. Au bas de l'avenue en falaise, les vagues courtes rendent le bleu de l'eau insoutenable comme un empâtement rêche de peinture. Devant, le pavillon du Yacht-Club, si noble, ces belles fenêtres Renaissance, ce quai long, ces quelques yoles sautillantes et, derrière, ce vague néant des prairies suburbaines entre les remblais de chemin de fer, comme un énorme bâillement de gueules vertes — avec ces beaux pylônes électriques entre lesquels les anges font de la corde raide chaque fois que le coup de canon du départ fait tourner la tête des spectateurs. C'est du joli.

Dans les salons de la Résidence de Calm Beach, le soir de la Redoute Fleurie, le scandale majestueux de cette partie de bridge où, mis au pied du mur sur une exorbitante enchère, un personnage en frac et masqué de noir, accoudé à ma gauche, à la dernière seconde glissa négligemment dans ma manche ce *neuf d'asperges* qui m'assurait le grand schlem.

Mes plus délicats souvenirs ? Ces soirées solitaires dans le rendez-vous de chasse de la Forêt Noire. Un grand feu de chapeaux-claque illuminait mes nuits, parfois, accoudé à un tesson de candélabre, je songeais : « Allons ! encore une nuit

Worldly Scandals

The day rises in a rain of warm lightning, greeted by bouts of maternal snowfall. The worker at the assembly line, skilled at counting the soft flow of minutes with his index finger, suddenly believes in a peculiar remission of his dream, and falls asleep. The connecting rods and transmission belts are suddenly blanketed with primroses. The world dozes off, with barely enough time to sneeze an *Ave Maria*.

This canal under the radiant February light. Below the cliffside avenue, the short-crested waves make the water's blue unbearable, like a painting's rough layering. Ahead, the Yacht Club's flag in all its dignity, these fine Renaissance windows, this long quay, these few bobbing wherries; behind, this vague emptiness of the outlying meadows between the rail embankments, like an enormous yawn of green mouths—with these fine pylons between which angels walk the tightrope every time a departure's gunshot makes heads turn. This is lovely.

In the parlors of the Calm Beach Residence, the night of the *Redoute Fleurie*, the majestic scandal of that game of bridge when, up against a wall after an outrageous bid, a figure in a tailcoat and black mask, leaning on his elbow to my left, at the last second casually slid into my sleeve that *nine of asparaguses*, which clinched the grand slam for me.

My most tender memories? Those solitary evenings in the Black Forest hunting lodge. A great fire of opera hats lit up my nights, at times, with my elbows on a glass candelabra shard, I'd think: "Come on! One more night of moonlight—let's all set sail from the Drum-Major's pier."

de clair de lune — on va s'embarquer en masse à la jetée du Tambour-Major. »

Dans les nuits claires du pôle, j'ai parfois chassé, rien que pour sentir sous mes doigts leurs détentes d'oiseaux, ces crevettes glacées et brûlantes qui remontent des cavernes d'ombre et s'agglutinent par grappes au bord des crevasses pour voir étinceler la Croix du Sud.

On clear nights at the pole, I've sometimes hunted, just to feel their birdlike ease beneath my fingers, those frozen, burning shrimp that arise from shadowy caverns and cluster at the edges of crevasses to see the Southern Cross sparkle.

La Rivière Susquehannah

Le long de la rivière Susquehannah roulent l'hiver des trains de marchandises, et les berges hollandaises sont une rangée de vide-bouteilles patronisés par les chauffeurs de locomotives avec leurs jolis bonnets de madapolam. Des ballets silencieux de patineurs parfois se dénouent devant la ventouse à l'haleine de perle d'un wagon engourdi par la neige sur sa voie de garage — mais d'un bout à l'autre de la journée l'impression dominante est un carillon de grosses cloches de bois. À midi, dans le blizzard et son coton saupoudré de suie, l'éclairage est une aube sibérienne indifférente, avec le choc des rondins coupés et le ronflement des manches de toile des elevators — des lointains indécis, à dix mètres, révèlent un homme d'équipe les mains dans les poches qui traverse en sifflotant une voie de garage. Les somnambules, à l'odeur de chien mouillé, sont groupés à l'écart dans une salle d'attente aveuglée par un poêle. Chacun paraît s'occuper peu de son voisin, et les allées et venues mal réveillées n'épouser qu'une convenance de pure forme, en l'attente de la cloche de six heures, comme au théâtre, avec les beaux groupes noirs mais qui s'éloignent dans la neige. Il y a aussi les hangars abandonnés où l'on boit des grogs fumants dans l'odeur de goudron et de sapins de Noël comme une gorgée de sciure de bois fraîche, et dans le terrain vague des voies les petits bars de panneaux démontables autour d'une chromolithographie qui représente Trotsky recevant les parlementaires allemands devant la gare de Brest-Litovsk.

Susquehanna River

Along the Susquehanna River freight trains run in the winter, and Dutch embankments are a row of taverns patronized by train drivers in their fine madapolam caps. Silent ballets of skaters sometimes unravel before the pearl breath exhaled by a freight car numbed by the snow on the sidetrack—but the day's dominant impression remains the chiming of large wooden bells. At noon, in the blizzard of soot-dusted cotton, the lighting is an indifferent Siberian dawn, with the shock of cut logs and the whirring of elevators' canvas shafts—in the hazy distance, ten meters away, a worker appears, hands in his pockets, whistling as he crosses a sidetrack. Sleepwalkers, smelling of wet dog, are gathered far away in a waiting room blinded by a stove. Everyone seems to care little for his neighbor, drowsily coming and going only as a formality, waiting for the six o'clock bell to ring, as in the theater, with fine black crowds drawing away into the snow. There are also abandoned barns that smell of tar and Christmas trees, where people sip steaming toddies like fresh sawdust, and, in the wasteland of the railroads, small bars with removable panels enclosing a chromolithograph of Trotsky receiving members of the German parliament in front of the Brest-Litovsk train station.

Bonne promenade du matin

À quelques encablures à peine de ma chambre, j'étais parfois surpris, à peine entamée ma promenade matinale, par des éclats dissonants de cuivre provenant d'une gracieuse maisonnette de briques en démolition. Sur les thèmes choisis de ce mystérieux orphéon des ruines, j'imaginais derrière cette façade de plâtras tristes toute une théorie de tonnelles ingénues et matinales, où des électriciens en cotte rouge, de blondes marcheuses des trottoirs de l'aube, des cortèges au sérieux travesti professionnel face au soleil levant dissipaient à part soi leurs brumes nocturnes dans quelques-unes de ces chopes d'étain ouvragées qui font si belle figure au premier plan d'une bacchanale d'opéra-comique. Se figure-t-on rien de plus charmant, avant le départ hâtif vers le travail sous les brandebourgs et les galaxies avenantes d'un bleu de chauffe, que le chœur rafraîchi de rosée, éventé de girandoles éteintes, qu'élèvent vers le soleil ces machinistes ingénus pour tout le jour condamnés à une dissimulation d'apaches dans les coulisses les plus poussiéreuses d'une ville moderne ? Un bal-minute, l'envol dans le chien et loup de l'aurore d'un jupon de dentelles, c'était la limite de ce que je pouvais imaginer des scandales de cette minuscule enceinte dissimulée aux arpenteurs de bitume par la retombée conventionnelle d'une courtine de plâtres promise aux trois coups du démolisseur. Mais déjà une jolie taverne de poutres mal équarries se permettait de faire chanter ses volets dans le soleil de l'aube, comme s'ouvrent les élytres matinaux des joyeuses bestioles des jardins. Déjà la rue m'appelait accueillante ; les pavés en grand arroi reprenaient leur place dans leurs alvéoles — rien, n'est-ce pas, ne s'était passé — et comme un loup sur le visage le plus troublant d'une femme aux débauches folâtres, après leur entrechat matinal les réverbères et les poubelles branlantes avaient repris leur faction de conserve sous l'œil militaire des balayeurs municipaux.

Pleasant Morning Walk

Just a few cable-lengths from my room, I was sometimes startled, my morning walk only just begun, by dissonant clashes of copper emerging from the demolition of a charming little brick house. Based on the chosen themes of that mysterious orphéon of ruins, I'd imagine behind that sad plaster facade a full procession of ingenuous morning arbors, where electricians in red overalls, blond streetwalkers at dawn, professional corteges in costume facing the rising sun dispersed nocturnal mists in a few of those finely wrought pewter tankards that look so lovely in the foreground of a comic-opera bacchanalia. Could anything more charming be imagined, before the morning rush to work in a uniform's froggings and pleasing galaxies, than the choir fresh with dew, fanned by extinguished girandoles, and raised toward the sun by those ingenuous stagehands condemned, for the entire day, to hide like delinquents in the dustiest wings of a modern city? A hasty ball, the flight of a lace petticoat in twilight's darkness was the limit of what I could imagine of the scandals behind that tiny enclosure hidden from land surveyors by the ordinary spring of a plaster curtain wall sure to be demolished in three strikes. But already a lovely tavern with uneven crossbeams was letting its shutters sing in dawn's light, like the elytra of happy garden bugs unfolding in the morning. Already the street was warmly beckoning me, the misaligned cobbles taking their places in their cells—nothing, isn't it so, had happened—and like a domino mask on a coquettish woman's most seductive face, after their morning *entrechat* the streetlamps and rickety trash cans had resumed their collective watch under the military eye of the city's sweepers.

Le Grand Jeu

Ce je ne sais quoi d'inconsistant qui flotte sur les quartiers proches des gares — la fécondité des grands nuages blancs de juin sur les prairies vertes, tout mangés d'azur sur les bords comme des veines bleues qui deviennent lait dans une mamelle — ce tendre glacis d'eau sur les yeux, sur les lèvres, cet ombilic de Vénus anadyomène par où baignera toujours pour moi dans quelle eau-mère la plus touchante des femmes — le hérissement soudain des eaux et des feuilles dans la lumière poudreuse d'un matin d'été brumeux le long des prairies couchées et des saules des grands fleuves — ce choc au cœur devant les paysages solennels de clairières, plus émouvantes entre les lisières de forêts rangées que le champ de bataille encore vierge, le concert prodigieux de silence qui sépare deux armées avant le chant de la trompette — ce tendre rose de fleur, cette effusion de pétales qui s'éveille au cœur du métal chauffé et rougit pour moi seul les grands drapeaux de tôle, l'estampage immaculé des arums et des lis — le crépuscule soudain, la *petite mort* mélancolique des cloches dans les après-midi écrasés de soleil des dimanches — les grands sphinx qui s'allongent au crépuscule sur les étangs brumeux des stades — le front à perte de vue sur les plaines d'un bois de légende comme le mur d'une cataracte de silence — aux douze coups de minuit le fantasme interdit d'un théâtre d'or et de pourpre, glacé, nacré, cloisonné, lamellé comme un coquillage, déserté comme une termitière après l'égorgement rituel, dans un maelström de pinces et de griffes, du couple royal — les délirantes géométries euclidiennes des gares de triage — les majestueuses processions de meubles d'un autre âge, les grands charrois de lits-clos des trains de marchandises — le

The Great Game

That fleeting je ne sais quoi floating above neighborhoods around train stations—above green meadows, the fertility of June's great white clouds eaten away at the edges by azure sky, like blue veins that become milk in a breast—that tender glaze of water on the eyes, on the lips, the navel of Venus Anadyomene in which there will always be, for me, bathing in mother water, the most touching of women—the sudden shiver of waters and leaves in the dusty light of a misty summer morning, along lounging meadows and willows by wide rivers—that heart-stopping moment before solemn landscapes of glades between clean forest edges, more moving than an untouched battlefield, the prodigious concert of silence that separates two armies before the trumpet's song—that tender pink of a flower, that effusion of petals that awakens at the heart of hot metal and reddens, for me alone, the large sheets of iron, the immaculate seal of arums and lilies—the sudden twilight, the melancholy *petite mort* of bells on Sunday afternoons oppressed by the sun—the great sphinxes lying on the hazy ponds of arenas at twilight—as far as the eye can see, the front on the plains in a wood of legend like the wall of a silent cataract—with the twelfth stroke of midnight, the forbidden fantasy of a gold and purple theater, icy, pearly, partitioned, bladed like a shell, deserted like a termite mound after the ritual slitting, in a maelstrom of pincers and claws, of the royal couple's throats—the delirious Euclidian geometries of marshaling yards—the majestic processions of furniture from another age, the freight trains' large cars with box-beds—the sovereign face, closed and sealed like a marble bust, of a middle-distance runner suspended over a bend, like a man on

visage souverain, clos et scellé comme un marbre, d'un coureur de demi-fond suspendu au-dessus d'un virage, comme un homme qui plonge à cheval dans la mer — le mancenillier abondant des lustres de Venise — le charme des forêts désaffectées des environs de Paris, où parfois un seul *château d'eau* veille sur d'immenses solitudes — j'ai parfois songé à *retourner* ces vignettes obsédantes, ces tarots d'un jeu de cartes fourbe — à chercher pour *qui* ces figures à jamais en moi singulières pouvaient n'avoir qu'un même envers.

horseback diving into the sea—the lush manchineel tree of
Venetian chandeliers—the charm of desolate forests in Paris's
environs, where sometimes a single *water tower* keeps watch
over expansive solitudes—at times I've thought of *turning over*
those haunting vignettes, those tarot cards of a duplicitous
game—to seek for *whom* those face cards, forever unique to
me, might have the same reverse side.

La Basilique de Pythagore

Il y a dans un coin de ma mémoire cette ville alerte dont je n'ai pas encore voulu jouir. Les boulevards tournent avec les rayons du soleil et l'ombre est de tout temps réservés aux rues de traverse et au quartier désuet des conspirateurs. C'est là que je m'achemine à midi sonné par des ruelles où le vent perpétuel rebrousse les herbes. De très vieux hôtels à baldaquins de pierre s'entremêlent çà et là à quelques-unes de ces charmantes gares de campagne désaffectées que la ville a avalées au passage — aussi bien conservées, ma foi, que Jonas dans sa baleine. Au coin de la rue se balance la pancarte bleue défraîchie de la salle d'attente des premières classes. Une maison hospitalière y donne — pourquoi pas ? — ses jeux folâtres ; par la grille du guichet il m'est donné parfois de surprendre, au creux d'un ballot de cotonnades, les ébats les moins condamnables. On se croit tout à coup — dans une apothéose de madras de couleur et cette ombre, cette ombre fraîche ! — au cœur de quelle Caroline du Sud ! Et la poussière ! — cette fine poussière de charbon des gares très patinées, dont l'odeur enivre. Tout autour, un jardin, accueillant — des colchiques, des bougainvilliers. Il est défendu de s'arrêter longtemps. L'ombre d'un gratte-ciel tout blanc éteint la petite gare, on pense tout à coup à la Sicile, aux rues en falaise de je ne sais quelle Salerne de béton où dans un ouragan de mouches l'ombre des loggias de l'Hôtel de ville haut perché écrase les maisons du port et leurs belles lingeries multicolores, leur grand pavois des jours de fête, qui sont tous les jours. Il y a aussi une débauche d'horloges de fer, comme de grandes araignées. Si débonnaires, si tranquilles. Le ferraillement énorme d'un tramway entre au cœur de tout cela comme un tremblement de terre,

The Basilica of Pythagoras

In a corner of my memory, there's a lively city whose pleasures
I have yet to desire. The boulevards turn with the sun's rays
and the shade is forever reserved for alleys and the deserted
neighborhood of conspirators. That's where I make my way, at
the sound of noon, through the little streets where the ever-
present wind brushes against the grass. Old hotels with stone
baldachins mingle here and there with those charming, rural
train stations that have since been swallowed by the city—now
disused but as enduring as Jonah in his whale. Swaying at the
corner of the street is the faded blue sign of the waiting room
for first-class passengers. There, a hospitable house is putting
on—why not?—its playful games; through the window's bars,
I've sometimes found, in the hollow of a cotton bale, revelry
of the least reprehensible kind. Suddenly one thinks oneself—
in a grand finale of colored madras and this shade, this cool
shade!—at the heart of some South Carolina! And the dust!—
this fine coal dust of weathered train stations, whose smell
is intoxicating. All around, a garden, welcoming—autumn
crocuses, bougainvillea. It is forbidden to stop for too long.
A white skyscraper's shadow extinguishes the small station,
Sicily suddenly comes to mind, or the cliffside streets of some
Salerno of concrete where, in a hurricane of flies, the shadow
of the town hall's loggias, perched high above, looms over the
houses by the port and their lovely multicolor linens, their
large flags raised on days of celebration, which is to say every
day. There's also an excess of iron clocks, like large spiders. So
debonair, so tranquil. A tramway's screech enters the heart of
it all like an earthquake, an explosion of dishes, or the joyful
racket of those tuned metal tubes rattled by doors opening

une explosion de vaisselle, ou le tintamarre réjouissant de ces tubes de métal accordés qu'ébranlent les portes des magasins pleins de pénombre où l'on marchande des bibelots d'osier, des porcelaines, des flacons treillissés de parfums exotiques. Pour en revenir à la petite gare, dans son jardin s'est réfugié un cèdre. Entre les murailles verticales qu'il touche et qui font sauter le cœur de joie à leur élan lisse, il étend ses branches comme ces niveaux d'eaux croupies des puits très profonds, les années de sécheresse. On a dû le descendre là au bout d'une corde, et c'est dans cette galerie de forage, sous ce culot de verdure, sous ces clapets de verdure dominés par cent trente-cinq étages et l'éclat neuf en plein jour de toutes les étoiles, c'est là que je donne mes rendez-vous d'amour et mes baisers voraces, mes premiers baisers.

into shadowy shops that sell wicker knick-knacks, porcelain, lattice bottles of exotic perfumes. To return to the small station, its garden offered refuge to a cedar. Between the walls it touches and whose smooth élan makes the heart leap with joy, it extends its branches like those stagnant water levels in deep wells during years of drought. We had to use a rope to climb down, and that vertical gallery, beneath the green base, beneath those green valves overlooked by 135 tiers and the new burst of stars in broad daylight, is where I go for my trysts and voracious kisses, my first kisses.

Les Jardins suspendus

Je suis entré dans la nuit fraîche des marronniers. C'est toujours vers les lisières des villes de province, à l'insertion soudaine des quartiers d'usines désaffectées où tremblent au vent des bouquets de filasse, des déchets de lingerie comme des pariétaires au long des grilles lépreuses des fenêtres, dans un silence plus prenant que celui d'une émeute avant le premier coup de feu, que j'aime à suivre au fil des basses voûtes noires ces traînées longtemps humides sur l'asphalte où tiédissent englués au sol les pétales blancs et roses, et ces lourdeurs humides de l'air sous le tunnel de branches le plus impénétrable que j'aie jamais vu. Le vide des pavés sur la droite, intercepté par la retombée des arbres, surprend comme une étendue marine et l'on peut cheminer seul selon la pente vers des rivières tristes, cimetière tout l'hiver des embarcations de plaisance, des places envahies silencieusement par les gazons et les jeux sans bruit des enfants pauvres, avec parfois un wagon de marchandises engourdi ou la vocalise dérisoire d'un cerf-volant. Rien ne me va davantage au cœur alors que la terrasse étouffée de verdures noires d'un café somnolent de ces boulevards excentriques. La solitude est celle des franges habitées d'où l'on tourne l'épaule aux fenêtres — comme du haut des falaises d'un vélodrome plein à craquer le regard étourdi jusqu'à l'écœurement qui flotte sur les terrains vagues où pend du linge à sécher aux guimbardes des nomades, ou le laisser-aller incompréhensible de somnolence des gares de triage de banlieue. Les heures glissant sans effort et sans trace sur le cadran plumeux d'un ciel océanique entre les feuilles, l'averse incolore et battante dont rien ne protège, la salle vide, le bâillement domestique submergeant sans effort le comptoir — quelle

Hanging Gardens

I entered the fresh night of chestnut trees. It's always toward
the edges of provincial towns, at the sudden introduction of
neighborhoods with disused factories, where clumps of oakum
and discarded linens tremble in the wind like pellitory along
leprous window grills, in a silence more riveting than that of a
riot before the first gunshot, that I like to follow, through the
low dark canopies, the trails of damp residue on the asphalt,
where white and pink petals glued to the ground begin to
cool, the air heavy and damp in the most impenetrable tunnel
of branches I've ever seen. The emptiness of the cobblestone
streets on the right, shaded by overhanging trees, takes one
by surprise like a marine expanse, and one can saunter alone
down the slope toward the sorrowful rivers, a cemetery of
pleasure boats in winter, squares invaded silently by grass and
the hushed games of poor children, and sometimes a sleeping
freight car or a kite's frivolous vocal exercise. Nothing touches
my heart more than a drowsy café terrace overgrown with
dark greenery on those outlying boulevards. Solitude comes
from the inhabited fringes from which one turns toward the
windows—like one's gaze, dizzy to the point of nausea, that
takes off from the heights of an overcrowded velodrome and
floats over deserted land where laundry hangs to dry from
nomads' caravans, or perhaps like the mystifying, drowsy lan-
guor of a suburban marshaling yard. The hours slipping by
effortlessly and without a trace on the feathery sundial of an
oceanic sky amid the leaves, the colorless, beating rain from
which nothing is protected, the empty room, the domestic
yawn effortlessly flooding the counter—a fine lull—and dizzy
from going nowhere along those singular ring roads, from the

halte ! — et vertigineusement, de n'aller à rien tout au long de ces singuliers boulevards de ceinture, du harassement dépaysant comme sous l'alizé de ces grands atolls de feuillages, sentir immobile circuler au flanc de la cité ce réseau de mort subite, et les grands coups de lance du désert jusques au cœur menacé des villes de ces tranchées familières du vent.

disorienting exhaustion caused by the trade winds of those grand atolls of foliage, one feels the web of sudden death encircling the city, along with those familiar trenches of wind, violent as the thrust of a spear, sweeping from the desert into the hearts of defenseless towns.

L'Appareillage ambigu

À minuit, par un clair de lune coupant comme un rasoir, je détachais l'amarre de la galère funèbre — et voguais. De longues étendues de terre plaine, des vols de ramiers blancs fantomatiques contre les berges, c'était le premier éveil de cette marine féerique que j'improvisais dans le creux du paysage nocturne. Solennels et funèbres, des chevaliers aux armures de sable me saluaient sur les berges du flamboiement fleurdelisé de leurs bannières — une haie d'oriflammes dessinait sur l'eau bleue comme du pétrole la carrière ouverte au triomphateur. À l'horizon, les vagues se perdaient dans de grands points d'orgue — parfois une trombe ardente, un gantelet de cristal, un doigt pointé comme l'index d'un cadran solaire figuraient le zodiaque familier de ces périples mal définis. À des fanaux soudain plus clairs, au branle-bas humide d'un appareillage nocturne, à mille feux Saint-Elme brillant sur les agrès, je pouvais déceler l'approche des brises du large comme le souffle d'une cave humide, puis c'était le coudoiement amical des pétroliers, d'immenses estacades de brumes, les balustrades géantes où s'accoudaient pour l'à-Dieu-vat les figurants majestueux avec leurs barbes de neige, leurs fracs et leurs éventails de théâtre, les éclaboussures salines et noires de suie où frissonnaient des épaules de marbre et, porté déjà sur l'encolure de la première houle et tout à coup en selle, le coup de clairon du lâchez-tout saluait le débordement de la jetée.

Ambiguous Departure

At midnight, under a moonbeam sharp as a razor, I untied the ropes of the mournful galley—and set sail. Long stretches of flat land and white, ghostly wood pigeons flying above the banks were the first awakenings of the magic seascape I improvised in the nocturnal scene. Solemn and mournful, knights in sable armor saluted me from the banks with the blaze of their banners' fleur-de-lis patterns—on the water blue as petrol, a row of oriflammes outlined the open course for the victor. Waves drew out in grand fermatas toward the horizon—at times a raging whirlwind, a crystal gauntlet, a finger pointing up like a sundial's gnomon served as the familiar zodiac for those ill-defined voyages. The beacons suddenly brighter, in the watery commotion of a nighttime departure, by the light of a thousand St. Elmo's fires shining on the rigging, I could discern the approach of the open sea breeze like the breath of a humid cellar, then there were oil tankers merrily rubbing shoulders, huge jetties of fog, giant balustrades where the majestic spectators with their snowy beards, tailcoats, and theatrical fans propped up their elbows and waited for the unmooring, the salty black soot splattering on shivering marble shoulders, and, the ship already carried by the first swell and suddenly mounted on its saddle, the bugle call to cast off greeted the flooding of the pier.

Paysage

Victime de ce singulier désœuvrement qui s'accorde à la chute du jour avec les fins de dîners solitaires, j'avais gagné ce soir-là la grande table d'orientation du cimetière de l'Ouest. Seuls peuvent rivaliser avec les sillons clairs des plaines à céréales, les avenues inégales creusées dans l'émotion passagère d'une Méditerranée, ces sérieux alignements de tombes enjambant les ondulations des collines qui se permettent, dans les faubourgs d'usines, d'engourdir parfois un coin du paysage sous leurs croûtes de pierre comme une Baltique sous ses banquises. C'était comme un sort jeté à la belle chevelure frissonnante de la planète par une gorgone des pâturages, les immobiles chardons de pierre, les chicots de granité, les troncs sciés à mi-corps, le champ d'abatis des chapelles funéraires meublant de leur bric-à-brac dément une clairière canadienne désertée par les défricheurs à l'heure où fume la bonne soupe du soir. Çà et là une hache oubliée, le grand arroi des pelles près d'une fosse fraîchement remuée ne laissaient pas que d'ajouter à l'illusion. Des buissons de ronces s'entrelaçant de traîtreux fils de fer, c'était aussi tout à coup toute la musique des bombardements, quand le paysage aéré, allégé par un souffle folâtre, laisse pour une minute un jeu plus libre aux règles de la pesanteur — enfin il n'était pas défendu, sans doute, de fourrager dans l'imprévu de ces curieuses poubelles, on s'étonnait même de l'absence frétillante autour des boîtes à ordures du caniche matinal. Quelque part, un clairon sonnait derrière une colline un remugle désenchanté de caserne, un de ces decrescendo solennels de cuivre qui s'accordent si bien à la croissance insouciante de l'herbe entre les pavés, des pâquerettes entre les tombes, et une petite revendeuse des faubourgs pourchassait au coin des stèles les premières violettes.

Landscape

Victim of that singular idleness harmonious with the end of a solitary dinner at the fall of day, that evening I had reached the grand orientation table of the West Cemetery. The furrows of wheat plains, the uneven avenues dug in a Mediterranean Sea's passing emotion, might be rivaled only by those imposing rows of tombs that cross undulating hills and numb, in the industrial districts, parts of the landscape under their stone crusts, like a Baltic Sea under its ice floes. It was as if a spell had been cast on the planet's lovely fluttering hair by a gorgon of the pastures—the immobile stone thistles, the granite stumps, the half-sawed trunks, the field of felled trees, mausoleums whose mad bric-a-brac furnished a Canadian glade deserted by land clearers in the evening, called away by a steaming, hearty soup. Here and there a forgotten axe, the large array of shovels near a freshly dug ditch only added to the illusion. Bramble bushes intertwining with traitorous wires—there was also suddenly the music of bombings, when the airy landscape, lightened by a playful breeze, momentarily allows for more leeway under the rules of gravity—it likely wasn't forbidden to rummage through the unexpected of that curious rubble, one was even surprised by the absence of the morning poodle wagging its tail around the trash cans. Somewhere behind a hill, a bugle sounded a disenchanting stench of barracks, one of those solemn, brassy decrescendos harmonious with the careless growth of grass between cobblestones, of daisies between graves, and a little tradeswoman from the neighborhood hunted around the headstones for the first violets.

La Justice

J'ai écouté les plaidoiries sans lassitude, parfois un tic nerveux dans l'épaule gauche. Une araignée au milieu du prétoire montait et descendait au bout de son fil, pareille au lustre compliqué des théâtres. Tout le monde, comprends-tu, saisissait l'allusion ; on aurait entendu voler une mouche. Les effets de manches des professionnels répandaient de grandes ondes d'un parfum d'amandes amères. Enfin j'ai trouvé ça particulier, je n'irai pas jusqu'à dire *sui generis*. Il y en a eu un à mort, trois à perpétuité, les autres se sont éclipsés sur la pointe du pied, avec de grands gestes de théâtre, derrière un trompe-l'œil élégant de volants de dentelles. Quand on a relevé le rideau pour la troisième fois, j'étais seul dans la salle à remercier le président, qui crachait des noyaux de cerises dans sa toque. Je te jure, c'était confondant.

Justice

I listened diligently to the pleas, at times with a nervous tic in my left shoulder. A spider in the middle of the courtroom crawled up and down its thread, like a theater's intricate chandelier. Everyone, you see, got the reference; you could have heard a fly buzz. The lawyers' grandstanding exuded strong waves of a bitter-almond scent. I found that, well, peculiar, but I won't go so far as to say *sui generis*. One was sentenced to death, three to life; the others tiptoed away with grand dramatic gestures, slipping behind an elegant trompe l'oeil of lace frills. When the curtain was raised for a third time, I was the only one in the room to thank the judge, who was spitting cherry pits into his cap. I swear, it was confusing.

La Vie de voyage

Nous quittions la ville vers trois heures du matin, quand les maisons ténébreuses des avenues se relancent de façade en façade les oiseaux de nuit, comme un tir aux pigeons de coussins de soie. L'aube se levait en ruban de lumière bleue sur les rails d'un tramway des faubourgs — mais, dès avant la terre promise, le ciel change ! c'est la pluie sur les vitrages d'un hôtel désaffecté de la plage, le déjeuner de pain gris sur lequel la mer fait le bruit des larmes. À qui s'en prendre ? tout désorientés, perplexes, nous faisons les cent pas sur l'estacade, en jetant nos morceaux de pain dans la mer. Voici : maintenant j'ai jeté sur mes épaules la pèlerine des pauvres, rattaché mes chaussures au coin amer d'une borne, et, tout seul maintenant sous la gargoulette des gouttières, j'attends l'heure de l'ouverture des épiceries.

The Traveling Life

We left town around three in the morning, when the avenues'
dark houses release night birds from facade to facade, like
silk-cushion targets in a game of clay-pigeon shooting. Dawn
rose in a ribbon of blue light above the tramway tracks in the
suburbs—but, just before the promised land, the sky changes!
Rain on the windows of an abandoned hotel by the beach,
brown bread for breakfast, where the sea makes the sound of
tears. Who is to blame? Disoriented and perplexed, we pace
back and forth on the pier, tossing our chunks of bread into
the sea. And now: I've thrown the poor man's cape over my
shoulders, tied my shoes around the bitter end of a bollard,
and, alone now under the gurglet of gutters, I wait for the
hour when grocery stores open.

Truro

Les flèches de la cathédrale de Truro sont maintenant deux
cônes de maçonnerie compacte, et l'aspect des façades a beau
demeurer le même, l'espace est étrangement mesuré aux
pièces habitées par l'épaississement anormal des murs ; quant
à la population — le sourire mesquin et tordu de quelqu'un à
qui on a marché sur le pied — on dirait d'un bernard-l'ermite
expulsé par une intumescence interne de sa coquille. Truro
souffre encore sans se plaindre. D'année en année, la crois-
sance de l'aubier minéral rétrécit vers l'intérieur des pièces l'es-
pace disponible ; en même temps la lutte sournoise du génie
végétal contre les angles vifs s'observe à plein : déjà nombre de
salles à manger sont en rotonde, et j'ai souvent, invité dans la
haute société de la ville, l'impression anachronique de pren-
dre le thé dans un donjon. Les meubles qu'on n'a pas eu la
précaution de mouvoir sont scellés aux murs par le progrès
de la gangue vitreuse, assez comparable par son aspect gan-
glionnaire à ces plaques muqueuses qui, de jour en jour, par
les hivers froids, bourgeonnent sur l'ardoise des urinoirs. La
minéralisation gagne particulièrement vite les draperies : l'as-
pect est resté encore souple que la main fait crouler les franges
des rideaux en une friable poussière de craie. On a beau éloi-
gner sa couche des murailles et cacher son appréhension sous
le prétexte de la mode ancienne *des lits de milieu*, il arrive par-
fois que le visiteur au petit matin tâte du doigt un drap déjà
rigide, ou crève d'un orteil impatient une insidieuse pellicule
de marbre, comme un poisson troue d'un coup de queue la
jeune glace des mers du Sud. Le phénomène des stalactites ne
s'observe guère que par les saisons pluvieuses, dans les parages
du Faubourg Maritime. Ce n'est pas qu'il y ait à proprement

Truro

The spires of Truro Cathedral are now two cones of compact masonry, and though the facades have remained the same, the space inside is constricted by an abnormal thickening of the walls, the population—with the sullen and twisted smile of someone whose toes have been stepped on—like a hermit crab evicted from its shell by an internal intumescence. Truro suffers without complaint. From year to year, the growth of mineral sapwood shrinks the rooms' available space; meanwhile, one can observe the vegetation's devious struggle against acute corners: already, numerous dining rooms have become rotundas, and when invited to join the city's high society, I often have the anachronistic impression that I am taking tea in a keep. The furniture no one had the foresight to move is fixed to the walls by the advance of glazed veinstone, whose ganglial appearance likens it to those mucus blotches that, from day to day, in cold winters, sprout over the slate stalls of public urinals. The mineralization has gained rather quickly on the draperies: they remain supple in appearance, but their fringe crumbles into powdered lime at the touch of a hand. Though some have pulled their beds away from the walls, hiding apprehension with claims of an earlier fashion of putting them *in the middle*, occasionally it comes to pass that in the morning a visitor's finger presses lightly against stiff sheets, or his impatient toe pierces a film of marble, like a fish's tail puncturing the young ice of the South Seas. The phenomenon of stalactites goes largely unobserved, except during rainy seasons in the Marine District. It's not that any of this is dangerous, strictly speaking, though there have been reports of subacute phenomena and cases of quickly occluded emergency exits,

parler danger, encore qu'on cite déjà des phénomènes subaigus et des cas d'occlusion accélérée des issues de secours, et cependant — quoique, je le reconnais, sans raisons *vraiment* péremptoires — je me permets de déconseiller dorénavant le séjour de Truro, car dans de telles pièces, comme dit le poète, on ne loge pas seulement son corps, mais aussi son imagination.

and yet—though not for any *truly* peremptory reasons, I recognize—from now on, I'll advise against a stay at Truro, for in such rooms, as the poet says, not only is one's body lodged, but also one's imagination.

Le Couvent du Pantocrator

Le couvent du Pantocrator sous les belles feuilles de ses platanes luit comme une femme qui se concentre avant de jouir. Le difficile est d'en tenter l'escalade et cependant ces chambres serpentant comme des méandres, ces toits où ruisselle l'huile du soleil, ces toits vernis, ces toits de beurre, ce labyrinthe de figuiers et de flaques de lumière à la pointe d'un précipice vertical, c'est cela seul qui m'attire et c'est là que s'orientent les voiles de cette tartane sur cette mer plate comme un bruit de ressac. Écoute la balancelle du vent sur les faîtages, du vent lent comme les vagues — puis c'est la pluie douce sur les carreaux treillissés de plomb, la pluie argentine, la pluie domestique entre les claires étagères à vaisselle et la niche familière du chien, c'est le couvent sur lequel tournent les heures, la grisaille des heures, la cloche des passe-temps, sur lequel les soleils tournent, et sur lequel la mer festonne ses vagues, la langue tirée, avec l'application d'une brodeuse, d'une Pénélope rassise et tranquille, d'une empoisonneuse de village entre ses fioles accueillantes et le pain qu'elle coupe à la maisonnée — le pain qui soutient et qui délasse — le pain qui nourrit.

The Convent of the Pantocrator

The convent of the Pantocrator under the lovely leaves of its plane trees glistens like a woman concentrating, on the verge of coming. The difficulty lies in climbing to the top, and yet these snaking rooms like winding rivers, these roofs where the sun's oil streams, these varnished roofs, these roofs of butter, this labyrinth of fig trees and puddles of light at the tip of a precipice, these alone draw me, and here this tartan's sails steer across this still sea like a sound of crashing swells. Listen to the swing of the wind on the roof ridges, the wind slow as waves—then there's the gentle rain on the lead-latticed windows, the silvery rain, the domestic rain amid glass-front cabinets and the dog's habitual corner, the convent where the hours turn, the hours' bleakness, the bell of pastimes, where the suns turn and the sea scallops her waves, sticking out her tongue with the focus of a woman embroidering, a seated and calm Penelope, a village poisoner among her inviting vials and the bread she slices for her household—the bread of sustenance and comfort—the bread of nourishment.

Au bord du beau Bendème

J'avais longtemps erré, aux heures déclinantes de l'après-midi, par les ruelles fraîches du quartier de cimetières et d'émeutes qui borde la cathédrale mixte. Une nonchalance appuyée, comme de doigts bagués qui tambourinent discrètement un coffre à bijoux dans la pénombre des beaux salons mérovingiens des antiquaires, à chaque spire de ce colimaçon aveugle de bâtisses alourdissait ma démarche. La prison d'air transparente colportait la sonorité des gongs. Le seul répit qui me fût accordé çà et là était celui de bancs vermoulus qui soulignaient les stations funèbres d'un *chemin de croix* blasonné d'enseignes romaines et de phalères, compliqué comme le canevas du métropolitain. De quel Calvaire borgne, de quelle Babel suburbaine ce labyrinthe était-il le piédestal ? Des portes parfois battaient avec mystère, mais c'était toujours au-delà d'un coude de la rue, et la poursuite décevante de ce sésame crapuleux des faubourgs m'excitait jusqu'à la démangeaison. Ces appels graves comme des cors, cette anxieuse poursuite à travers des clairières de gravats, des échafaudages d'échelles, tout un Hoggar calciné de boutiques aveugles m'amenèrent soudain, derrière les tamis d'une pluie fine, en présence de l'*abside* du bâtiment le plus ambigu qu'il m'ait été donné de voir, — me glissèrent le mot de passe qui neutralisait la sentinelle de la poterne, et sous les gros fanaux lisses et glauques des vitraux, les larmes aux yeux je me sentis fondre jusqu'à mi-corps dans l'herbe musculeuse et chevelue d'une prairie océanique.

On the Banks of Fine Bendemeer

I had wandered a long while, in the fading hours of the afternoon, through the cool streets in the neighborhood of cemeteries and riots near the mixed-style cathedral. A pronounced nonchalance, like that of ringed fingers drumming discreetly on a jewelry box in the penumbra of antiquarians' elegant Merovingian salons, made my step heavy with each turn in the blind spiral of buildings. The transparent prison of air spread the sound of gongs. The only respite given me now and then came from worm-eaten benches that evoked the funereal *stations of the cross* blazoned with Roman emblems and phalerae, as complex as the metro's canvas. This labyrinth seemed to serve as pedestal for some shadowy Calvary, some outlying Babel. Doors swung mysteriously here and there, though always beyond a bend in the road, and the dismal pursuit of that sordid opening to the outskirts excited an itching desire within me. Those calls deep as horns, that anxious pursuit through heaps of rubble, ladder scaffoldings, rows of blind shops barren as the Hoggar Mountains, suddenly brought me, behind the screens of a fine rain, before the *apse* of the most ambiguous building I've ever seen—then slid me the password that neutralized the sentry at the postern, and under the wide beams of light, smooth and sea-green from the stained glass windows, with tears in my eyes, I felt the lower half of my body melt in the vigorous, tufted grass of an oceanic meadow.

Le Passager clandestin

Quelquefois j'étais transporté sur un rivage démesuré de ville glorieuse, enverguée à l'air de ses mille mâts, criant dans l'air comme un geyser éteint ses cris figés de pierre, une pyramide haute de murs à la patine soyeuse où dans les rues du soir se prenait comme une glace au-dessus de la banquise de la mer le cristal noble de l'air sonore, et très loin par-delà les hautes murailles des trompettes calmes sans cesse protégeaient une solennité mystérieuse — un port du large lavé des vents et dévasté par une mer où plongeaient rouge les soleils rapides, et là, couché au bout d'un môle, au ras des vagues penchées toutes et courant bouclées d'un seul souffle emportant — sur mes épaules, les tours et les dômes dorés fumants d'une poussière de soleil dans le bleu exténué sous le harnais de la journée chaude — fasciné par un songe salé d'embrun solaire et sur mon dos l'énorme gonflement de bulles de ces carapaces séculaires, les corridors de crime de ces millions d'alvéoles, les places désertes autour des statues de gloire et des spectres du grand jour, les porches des palais aveugles empanachés noir d'un claquement ténébreux d'oriflammes, comme un homme qui crie en plein midi — la ville aspirée avec moi dans le miroir débordant du soir se déhalait sur la mer dans un grésillement de braise, fendait l'eau d'une poitrine monstrueuse sous ses colonnes de toile, sur une houle de rumeurs et de silence, sous le brouillard de lumière vivante et le buisson ardent de ses drapeaux.

The Stowaway

Sometimes I'd be transported to the vast shore of a glorious city, its sails bent to the yards of its thousand masts, letting into the air its petrified cries like an extinct geyser, a tall pyramid of silky patina walls where, in the evening streets, the noble crystal of the ringing air formed like frost above an ice floe, and far in the distance beyond the high walls, calm trumpets guarded a mysterious solemnity—a port cleansed by winds, devastated by a sea where rapid suns sunk red, and lying there at the end of a pier, level with the tilting, curly waves swept forth by a single gust—on my shoulders, the golden towers and domes smoking with sun-dust in the exhausted blue under the warm day's harness—enchanted by a salty dream of solar ocean spray and on my back the enormous bubble-like bulge of those ancient carapaces, the corridors of crime among those millions of cells, the deserted squares around statues of glory and ghosts in broad daylight, the porches of blind palaces plumed and black with dark flapping oriflammes, like a man crying out at midday—the overflowing mirror of the evening breathed me in along with the city that hauled out to sea in a crackling of embers, splitting the water with its monstrous chest under canvas columns, on a swell of murmurs and silence, under the fog of vibrant light and the burning bush of its flags.

Cortège

Hommes 40 — chevaux 8, à cette seule inscription régle-
mentaire s'annonçait de loin — dans l'attente de marques
plus expressives de la glorieuse résurrection — le boggie
mortuaire — non sans qu'eussent défilé en belle ordon-
nance — seulement ralentis pour un moment par l'escalade
de la rampe — les salons de première classe où les bijoux de
jais étincelaient aux doigts des jolies bridgeuses — en train de
tuer le temps que concrétisait seulement d'un moment à l'au-
tre — celui que le *mort* voulût bien consacrer à jouer enfin
cartes sur table — le coup d'œil jeté à travers la portière sur
l'étendue mouvante et pluvieuse d'un paysage indifférent.

Cortege

Men 40—horses 8, bearing this official inscription alone, there presented itself in the distance—in expectation of more expressive signs of the glorious resurrection—the funereal bogie— not before there passed in fine succession—slowed only for a moment by the ramp's incline—the first-class lounges where jet jewelry sparkled on the fingers of pretty bridge players— killing time that was concretized only in the next moment— time the *dead man* would have liked to spend laying all his cards on the table—by the glance cast through the car door on the shifting and rainy expanse of an indifferent landscape.

La Bonne Auberge

Les hommes sont coupés à mi-hauteur par la guillotine de l'habit noir — les femmes prennent sous le baiser la vibration tranchante du cristal, puis éclatent et sèment sous la neige d'adorables camélias de sang. On décharge successivement sur le perron d'entrée avec un bruit de fardiers le landau du lord-maire : roses-thé et héliotropes — le mail-coach de la magistrature : fouet et roues en réséda — la voiture tous terrains de la préfecture des mœurs : hortensias et jonquilles. Et maintenant que faire ? les couples noués, les présentations terminées, les revolvers sortent des poches et la fête commence dans un tir aux pigeons flamboyant de verre cassé. À l'aube louche, les habits noirs, mal à l'aise, s'esquivent deux par deux comme des croque-morts dans les sentiers de feuilles — les planchers désertés étalent une Bérésina de fins débris de verre ; les plantes vertes : des arbres de Noël de neige craquante et de verre filé — plusieurs âmes blanches gagnent les hautes régions du ciel sous la forme de délicats petits anges — légères comme une inconséquence dans un problème de métaphysique. On préfère ne savoir que penser d'une désinvolture qui désarme jusqu'aux soupçons de la justice.

The Good Inn

Men are cut in half by the guillotine of their tailcoats—with a kiss, women absorb the crystal's sharp vibration, then burst and sow charming blood camellias beneath the snow. With the sound of drays, vehicles unload one by one before the entrance—the lord-mayor's landau: tea roses and heliotropes—the magistrature's mail-coach: whip and mignonette wheels—the vice squad's all-terrain carriage: hydrangeas and daffodils. And now what? Couples knotted, introductions over, revolvers emerge from pockets and the festivities begin with a show of flying glass shards, like targets in a game of clay-pigeon shooting. In dawn's haze, the men in tailcoats grow ill at ease, slip away in pairs like morticians on the leafy paths—a Berezina of fine glass fragments spreads across the deserted floors; the green plants: Christmas trees of crunchy snow, drawn glass—several white souls rise to the sky's heights in the form of delicate little angels—light as an inconsistency in a metaphysical problem. An ease so disarming as to allay justice's suspicions may best be left unconsidered.

Surprises-parties de la maison des Augustules

Les trottoirs, ce matin-là, sont des escaliers de fontaines pétri-
fiantes où fument dans la perspective de beaux alignements
de cataractes. Aucun souffle de vent, mais à perte de vue
sur les boulevards on entend casser une à une les branches
des marronniers avec un bruit de mousqueterie. De temps à
autre, quelques reliures à armoiries font explosion dans les
éventaires des quais de la Seine — des gousses géantes en-
trent en déhiscence sur le zinc des estaminets. Partout des
visages de bois ; la journée s'annonce rude ; sur la Montagne
Sainte-Geneviève, par intervalles, on signale une grêle serrée
de boules de bleu à lessive. L'aube à peine levée, l'affluence
des facteurs est à Saint-Julien-le-Pauvre, cependant que Saint-
Nicolas-du-Chardonnet coagule le menu peuple de la blanchis-
serie — à Saint-Germain-l'Auxerrois, derrière l'autel, on tire le
canon, méthodiquement, toutes les vingt secondes. C'est à ne
plus s'entendre, cela tourne au scandale : à chaque détonation
l'archevêque fait s'envoler des pigeons de sa manche. Des ga-
zelles sortent en foule des maisons closes et se rassemblent sur
les parvis municipaux.

Parties at the House of Augustulus

At dawn, the sidewalks are stairs of petrifying fountains where fine alignments of waterfalls smoke into the distance. No wind gusts, but on the boulevards, as far as the eye can see, branches of chestnut trees can be heard cracking one by one, a sound of musketry. Occasionally, a few book bindings with coats of arms explode in the stalls along the quays of the Seine; giant seed pods split and land on the zinc counters of small cafés. Wooden faces everywhere. A difficult day lies ahead. On the hill at Montagne Sainte-Geneviève, a dense hail of balls of bluing is reported intermittently. The sun scarcely risen, masses of mailmen are at Saint-Julien-le-Pauvre, while Saint-Nicolas-du-Chardonnet clumps together laundry service workers; at Saint-Germain-l'Auxerrois, behind the altar, the cannon is fired methodically, every twenty seconds. Drowning out all conversation, it turns into a scandal: with each detonation, the archbishop releases pigeons from his sleeve. Gazelles leave brothels in crowds and gather before churches in the city's squares.

La Vallée de Josaphat

Le paysage au fil de la route, comme au fil d'une flèche son empennage. Je suis seul. L'auberge vide où les pas résonnent sur le carreau des déluges. Une bouteille tinte, les bruits s'engluent, le temps coule en cahots boiteux, puis oublie de couler. Le bon lit de la terre fraîche rabat les gestes pauvres. Le tintement solennel de l'eau. Le verre s'est refermé sur la table comme sur la huche son couvercle. Sous une brume de glèbe fauchée, on entend couler le fleuve de la route mystérieuse. Dormir, la tête sur la table, au centre de la ronde de fraîcheur.

Les yeux bougent comme le tournesol et l'héliotrope et sur les ruisseaux de lait du crépi de la chambre se diluent dans la tache d'encre d'un papillon noir.

The Valley of Josaphat

The landscape along the road, like the fletching along an arrow. I am alone. The empty inn where footsteps echo on the tiles like rain. A bottle rings, sounds stick together, time flows in fitful lurches, then forgets to flow. The bed of fresh earth takes in feeble movements. The solemn tinkling of water. The glass has closed over the table, like the lid over a bread bin. In a mist fresh as reaped grass, one hears the flowing river of the mysterious road. Sleeping, head on the table, amidst a spiral of wind.

Eyes move like sunflowers and heliotropes and, on the milky streams of the bedroom's roughcast, dissolve in the ink stain of a black butterfly.

La Terre habitable

The Habitable Earth

Paris à l'aube

Il y a dans toute trajectoire un passage à vide qui retient le cœur de battre et écartèle le temps : celui où la fusée, au sommet amorti de sa course, se pose sur le lit de l'air avant de s'épanouir — où le gymnaste entre deux trapèzes, un instant interminable, appuie notre diaphragme à un vide de nausée — *une perte de vitesse* où la ville qu'on habite, et que recompose pour nous jour après jour, comme ces larves de lenteur qui flottent sur la moire d'une hélice, l'accélération seule, le volant lancé à fond d'un maelström d'orbites folles, se change en fantôme rien qu'à laisser sentir un peu son immense corps. Le jour qui se lève sur Paris n'a pas affaire avec l'exultation de la planète, avec le lever de soleil orchestral de la Beauce ou de la Champagne : il est le reflux aveugle d'une marée interne du sang — il est l'affleurement sur un visage vivant, à la surface d'une vie close, d'un signe de secrète et rongeante fatigue — l'heure où la vie se retire vers sa laisse la plus basse et où les moribonds s'éteignent — il est ce moment poignant, cette heure douteuse, où d'une tête aimée sur l'oreiller le visage *s'envole*, et, comme à un homme qui marche sur la neige, un masque inconnu s'oriente selon l'éclairage incomparable de la mort.

Ce cœur a beaucoup battu, et connaît maintenant que tant de beauté est mortelle. Il y eut des matins où, au fond des brumes du lit, le premier claquement amical d'un volet sur les ténèbres était la veilleuse rassurante qui brille toujours à la fenêtre d'un malade en danger — où les rues noires étaient les intervalles douteux d'une flotte à l'ancre d'étraves sourcilleuses, et où l'écho rassurant des pas sur l'asphalte ne pouvait donner le change sur son aptitude découverte à l'engloutissement. Dans l'air acide de l'aube qui se lève sur Paris, il

Paris at Dawn

In every trajectory there's a moment of suspension that keeps the heart from beating and divides time: when a firework, at the softened summit of its course, settles on a bed of air before blossoming—when a gymnast between two trapezes, in an endless instant, presses our diaphragm into a nauseating emptiness—*a loss of momentum* when the city we inhabit, reconstructed for us day after day by acceleration alone, like sluggish larva floating on a propeller's shimmering surface, steering wheel thrown into a maelstrom of chaotic orbits, turns into a ghost, simply by allowing a trace of its immense body to be felt. Daybreak in Paris has nothing to do with the planet's jubilation, with the symphonic sunrise in Beauce or Champagne: it's the blind ebb of an inner tide of blood—it's the outcrop on a vigorous face, on the surface of a sheltered life, of a secret, gnawing fatigue—the hour when life recedes to its lowest foreshore, when the dying fade away—it's that poignant moment, that shadowy hour when the face *takes flight* from the beloved head on the pillow, and an unknown mask, like a man trudging through snow, gets its bearings in death's incomparable light.

This heart has beaten a long while and knows now that so much beauty is mortal. There were mornings when, deep in the layers of mist, a shutter slamming pleasantly over the darkness was as reassuring as the ever-shining night light by the window of a deathly sick man—when the dark streets were the dubious intervals between an anchored fleet's imposing ships, and when the reassuring echo of footsteps on asphalt couldn't hide its aptitude for engulfment. In the bitter air of Paris at dawn, in the empty streets, when the day's first

traîne encore aujourd'hui par les rues vides, au pas du premier promeneur, quelque chose du coup de talon rude du marin qui éprouve le pont de son navire — il fond dans la bouche avec la première lampée d'air un goût de pain quotidien. La ville se dresse, ailée, effilochant son cocon de brumes jaunes, deux fois émouvante de sa force et de sa fragilité.

Quiconque traverse Paris avant que ne se lève le jour traverse avec gêne un chantier engourdi en pleine marche, qui appelle instantanément l'herbe folle, une machinerie géante débrayée brutalement par le sommeil de l'œil et de la paume de l'homme, et déjà insensiblement érodée, ravalée à l'état panique de paysage par je ne sais quelle housse de pesanteur. Un désert à perte de vue de murs, de chaussées luisantes, et de miroirs d'eau claire propose chaque matin aux hommes la tâche exténuante de le fleurir tout entier, de le vêtir et de l'*aveugler* — comme ces maisons abattues qu'une palissade si exactement remplace — , d'une toile sans couture de circuits, de trajectoires et de rumeurs. Dans ces échafaudages machinés, ce labyrinthe de pistes luisantes, ces entassements de colonnes, le matin, comme un flot qui se retire, décèle à un troublant manque de réponse ce caractère de provocation pure à une activité incompréhensible qui demeure à une capitale aussi secret, aussi essentiel qu'à une femme la nudité. Cette heure aventureuse où Rastignac, du haut du Père-Lachaise, répond au défi, est en vérité une heure interdite. Un peuple entier a sécrété une carcasse à sa mesure monstrueuse pour y plaquer à bout de bras de toute sa hauteur la robe de ses millions de désirs. L'œil sacrilège qui glisse à travers la nudité grelottante d'une aube dans les rues de Paris surprend quelque chose du scandale d'un fond de mer entrouverte, de cet instantané plein de malaise d'une coupure encore exsangue que le sang dans une seconde va combler jusqu'à son bord. Une grêle rude de caresses s'apprête à fondre sur cette vacance amoureuse : le labyrinthe béant d'un ventre endormi et découvert féminise la

ambler sets foot outside, there remains something of the harsh heel strike of a sailor inspecting the deck beneath his feet—a taste of daily bread melts in his mouth with his first gulp of air. The city rises, with wings, unravelling its cocoon of yellow mist, all the more moving for its strength and fragility.

Whoever walks through Paris before daybreak cautiously weaves through a numbed construction site overgrown with weeds, a giant cluster of machinery suddenly disengaged by man's sleepy eyes and palms, slowly eroding and returning to the chaotic state of landscape by who knows what shroud of heaviness. As far as the eye can see, a desert of walls, gleaming roadways, and clear-water mirrors presents men every morning with the demanding task of reviving it, of clothing and *blinding* it—like those demolished houses replaced so meticulously by a hedge—with a seamless web of circuits, trajectories, and murmurs. In those scaffoldings, that labyrinth of gleaming paths, those heaps of columns, the morning, like a receding wave, reveals to a troubling silence that sense of pure provocation characteristic of an elusive activity as secret and essential to a capital city as nudity is to a woman. That adventurous hour when Rastignac, from the top of Père-Lachaise, responds to the challenge is, indeed, a forbidden hour. An entire people has secreted a carcass of monstrous proportions, which they use all their strength to cover with the cloak of their endless desires. The sacrilegious eye gliding through dawn's shivering nudity in the streets of Paris discovers something of the scandal of a cracked seabed, of that moment of malaise when blood is on the verge of spurting past the edges of a cut. A harsh hail of caresses soon melts over this romantic vacancy: the wide-open labyrinth of a dozing, exposed belly feminizes the city, hangs the springs of a tireless erethism from its secret caves, draws the hungry and solitary into its streets at the crack of dawn, and gives a morning stroll the absorbing, guilty character of possession.

ville, accroche à ses grottes secrètes les ressorts d'un éréthisme inlassable, attire dans ses rues à la première heure l'affamé et le solitaire, et communique à la flânerie matinale le caractère absorbant et coupable de la possession.

Il y a une ivresse trouble à traverser, tremblante à l'extrême bord du repos nocturne, cette frange baudelairienne du « rêve parisien » où la ville, rédimée de toute servitude, s'engrène une minute aux formes pures de l'espace et du temps, où le long des failles lisses des rues comme dans un port saccagé s'égalise la marée des brumes, et où la cité, entraînée au fil de son fleuve, écoute maniaquement sonner l'heure aux horloges plus attentives, dans cette majesté fascinante qui rebâtit de marbre une capitale à la veille d'un tremblement de terre. Le corps géant s'est dépris une fois de plus d'un coup de reins dédaigneux de tout ce qui le manie, comme une divinité aux yeux vides et bleuâtres qui se recouche, à nouveau déserte, pour peser sur l'horizon d'un poids pur. L'étrangeté inabordable de la forêt vierge en une nuit revient expulser l'homme de l'ouvrage de ses mains. Les yeux qu'on frotte clignent une seconde sur le gel de cette nécropole pétrifiante, une main secourable empoigne les outils, le soleil libéré d'un million d'énergies refoule à ses brouillards le fantôme d'une lucidité inhumaine, un sang tumultueux et confiant bouillonne à tous les canaux, ouate un timbre de mort, brouille des perspectives inexorables, une face aveugle et sourde, médusante, se dilue dans le jour qui monte avec les étoiles : pour Paris, comme pour la sentinelle biblique, le matin vient, et la nuit aussi.

There is a blurry intoxication to be traversed, trembling at the extreme edge of a night's rest, this Baudelairian fringe of the "Parisian dream" where the city, released from all constraints, is momentarily engaged with the pure forms of time and space, where along the streets' smooth cracks, as in a pillaged port, the tide of mists evens out, and where the city, swept along its river, listens intently to the chiming hour on the more attentive clocks, in this enchanting majesty that rebuilds a capital in marble the day before an earthquake. The giant body has broken free once more, with a disdainful thrust, from all that controls it, like a blue-eyed deity with a blank stare who, deserted once more, lies back down to burden the horizon with her sheer weight. A virgin forest's impenetrable strangeness returns at night to expel man from the work of his hands. Rubbed eyes blink for a second at this petrifying necropolis, a helping hand grabs hold of tools, the sun breaks free and shoves the inhumanly lucid ghost back into its fog, a bold, tumultuous stream of blood boils through every channel, muffles the tone of death, blurs clear views, a blind and deaf face, paralyzing, dissolves in the day that rises with the stars: for Paris, as for the biblical sentinel, morning comes, and so does night.

L'Explorateur

J'ai vécu de peu de choses comme de ces quelques ruelles vides
et béantes en plein midi qui s'ensauvageaient sans bruit dans
un parfum de sève et de bête libre, leurs maisons évacuées
comme un raz-de-marée sous l'écume des feuilles. Pareilles à
ce panache de l'explosion d'une poudrière qui dégonfle une
ville, de grandes masses de verdure orageuse roulaient un ciel
sombre au-dessus des toits crevés. L'après-midi me retrouve
devant un haut mur de parc aveugle, tendant l'oreille, comme
on surprend un bruissement de feuilles derrière une porte.
À l'air libre, trempé soudain de soleil tournoyant comme
par une fanfare, mes pieds amoureusement ravivant la pente
secrète d'une colline longue comme une joue, je redescen-
dais chaque soir aux champs calmes, les mains pleines comme
celui qui touche une femme, appuyant le front encore, les
yeux fermés, ainsi que le cœur manque et qu'on marche en
dormant, au songe odorant et au vide sous le soleil de ce vil-
lage accoudé à la forêt comme un après-midi d'été au balcon
de sa nuit sauvage.

The Explorer

Little has sustained me more than some of those empty narrow streets yawning at midday and silently growing wild amid a scent of sap and free-roaming animals, their houses evacuated like a tidal wave beneath the froth of leaves. Like the smoke from the explosion of a powder magazine that flattens a town, masses of stormy greenery rolled a dark sky over the punctured roofs. The afternoon finds me before a park's high blind wall, listening closely, as if to discern a rustling of leaves behind a door. In the open air, suddenly soaked in sunlight twirling like a fanfare, my feet lovingly reviving a secret hillside long as a cheek, I'd come down every evening back to the calm fields, hands full like a man touching a woman, still pressing against my forehead, eyes closed, as they are in a waking sleep and when the heart aches, back to a fragrant dream, to the emptiness under the sun of that village leaning against the forest like a summer afternoon against the balcony of its wild night.

Moïse

Les yeux fermés sous les feuilles fraîches de ses troènes, le chemin d'eau m'emportait chaque après-midi à reculons comme une Ophélie passée dans sa bouée de fleurs, dissolvant lentement du front les clôtures molles. Couché plus bas qu'aucune autre créature vivante sur l'oreiller fondamental, tombait sur moi la face des arbres comme la rosée d'un visage penché sur un lit de malade, et mettant le monde doucement à flot sur ma route comme un liège, j'étais fiancé aux anneaux sonores des ponts comme une gaze, de plain pied avec le mufle bénin des vaches. L'ombre de la forêt sur la rivière mêlait à l'eau noire une douce tisane de feuilles mortes et d'oubli. Midi me trouvait dérivant au large ensoleillé de vastes grèves scintillantes, les mains closes sur le cœur, les paupières éclatantes de langueur, puis le somptueux froissement des roseaux dévorait les rives d'une palissade théâtrale de murmures, et mollement entravé comme d'une robe par les tiges aux longues traînes, engourdi au fond d'une impasse verte, les doux maillons de soleil de l'eau qui me portait comme un ventre, comme un qui regarde au fond d'un puits redescendaient jusqu'à moi en se dénouant sur le visage d'une femme.

Moses

Eyes closed under fresh privet leaves, the water path carried me backwards every afternoon like a pale Ophelia in her buoy of flowers, the waves slowly dissolving the soft enclosures. I lay on the elemental pillow, lower than any other living creature, the aspect of trees falling on me like the dew of a face leaning over a sickbed, and setting the world sweetly afloat on my path like a cork, I was betrothed to the bridges' resounding rings like gauze, level with the harmless muzzles of cows. The forest's shadow on the river mixed the black water with a sweet tisane of dead leaves and forgetfulness. Noon found me drifting on the sunlit sea of vast scintillating shores, hands closed over my heart, eyelids bursting with languor, as the reeds' sumptuous rustling ate away at the banks of a theatrical hedge of murmurs, and, gently entangled in the stalks like a dress with long trains, numbed in the depths of a green dead end, I was carried by the water like a belly, the sweet nets of sunlight descending over me like a man gazing into the depths of a well, unraveling over a woman's face.

Roof-garden

Sur le rempart il y a un petit champ vert où poussent les
églantines, les ravenelles, et les avoines de la nouvelle journée.
Parfois coulant comme un fleuve jaune, parfois un écheveau
sous des ongles d'air, parfois la paille douce d'une chevelure
blonde prise dans un rouet. Avec le soir, les chaumes sont un
reposoir où montent les fumées charmantes de la ville comme
les corolles d'un bombardement de fête et de silence, et par
les archères on voit le ciel écumer de nuages légers et les cam-
pagnes comme la poitrine d'une femme sous l'énorme chaleur.
On épierre le champ à même sur le vide et la carapace des
toits, et il y a des chemins couverts et des routes douces dans
les herbes, les pierres, et la forêt balsamique des orties jusqu'à
la plate-forme rase où le ciel sur la mer de paille est un orage
mexicain, où l'air coule comme de l'huile dans la gueule d'un
canon de bronze, et l'herbe folle au-dessus du fleuve frissonne
sans cause comme l'épaule d'un cheval.

Roof Garden

On the rampart there's a little green field where sweetbriars, wild radishes, and oats grow in the new day. Now flowing like a yellow river, now a skein under fingernails of air, now the soft straw of blond hair caught in a spinning wheel. With evening, the thatches become an altar where the town's charming smoke rises like the corollas of a festive explosion of silence, and through the loopholes one can see the sky's light, frothy clouds and the land like a woman's chest under the unbearable heat. The field's stones are thrown into the void and over the roofs, and covered ways and sweet roads wind through the grasses, stones, and balsamic forest of nettles until they reach the low platform where the sky over the sea of straw is a Mexican storm, where the air flows like oil in a bronze cannon's mouth, and the wild grass above the river shudders unprompted like a horse's shoulder.

Intimité

C'est l'heure de la rentrée des vignes et des abreuvoirs, l'heure dernière. Les puits sont vides, et il y a une fourrure de tourterelles au bord des hangars, un liséré de satin comme une neige rouge aux très anciens costumes qui se penchent aux croisées, sous ces nuques d'oiseaux de proie — sous les porches battants passent des vents étrangers, qui sentent les chaumes et les palmes — les chars s'encapuchonnent — on a froid ici — des odeurs creusent des faims étranges sous les tilleuls et les abeilles, des pains dorés fléchissent les tables de la cuisine. On entend des clameurs et des appels très tard, du côté des clairières rouges, au large de la maison vide où chante la bouilloire oubliée sur les braises calmes. Le sommeil des persiennes sur l'aquarium de la chambre basse ranime doucement le globe aux fleurs d'orange comme un œuf nocturne au creux des chaumes, la main qui tisonne le loquet de fer, l'horloge qui éclabousse l'enclume du silence. Le marécage et le clair de lune brouillé des étables festonnent la nuit fleurie qui monte du creux des armoires, le parfum de grotte et de suaire moisi, le terrier rêche du lit de ménage, la nudité mystique de l'épouse auprès du lis consolateur des nuits noires.

Intimacy

It's the hour of return from vineyards and troughs, the final hour. The wells are empty, and there's a lining of turtledoves by the barns, a satin trim like a strip of red snow on old garments lying by the windows, beneath the napes of raptors—under the rattling porches pass foreign winds, smelling of straw and palms—the wagons are covered—it's cold here—smells rouse strange hungers under the lime trees and honeybees, golden loaves bend the kitchen tables. One hears clamors and calls late at night, by the red glades, distant from the empty house where the kettle whistles, forgotten on the calm embers. The sleeping shutters over the aquarium of the lower bedroom softly revive the orange-blossom orb like a nocturnal egg nestled in straw, the hand prodding the iron latch, the clock tarnishing the anvil of silence. The swamp and the stables' misty moonlight adorn the blooming night that rises from within the wardrobes, the scent of a cave and musty shroud, the rough burrow of the domestic bed, a bride's mystical nudity beside the consoling lily of black nights.

Les Hautes Terres du Sertalejo

À Jules Monnerot

Il me suffit de fermer les yeux pour que revienne le souvenir de cette saison légère où nous vagabondions, Orlando et moi, par les hautes terres du Sertalejo. Je revois les cieux balayés, d'une clarté lustrale de grève lavée, où les nuages au dessin pur posaient des volutes nacrées de coquillages — les longues pentes vertes basculées au-dessus des abîmes, où les doigts du vent plongeaient dans les hautes herbes — les lacs de montagne, serrés au cœur de l'étoilement dentelé des cimes comme un peu d'eau de la nuit au creux d'une feuille. Mais par-dessus tout, avec la fascination d'un accord longuement tenu où courent se noyer comme en une eau dormante les arabesques de la mélodie, revient me hanter le silence : un silence de haute lande, de planète dévastée et lisse où rien n'effrange plus sur le sol les ombres des nuages, et où la lumière du soleil éclate dans le tonnerre silencieux d'une floraison.

Nous avancions par courtes étapes, car dans ces plateaux la fatigue tombe soudain comme un manteau de plomb sur les épaules, et l'air raréfié des hautes altitudes nous enfiévrait le cœur. Nous nous mettions en route au petit matin, où l'air sentait la neige et l'étoile et mordait le ventre — nous replions les tentes et nettoyions les fusils. Nous cheminions quelque temps côte à côte, ranimés par la bonne conversation du matin, puis un étranglement de la piste, un défilé pierreux nous disjoignait — les paroles se faisaient plus rares — et le silence retombait sur notre maigre file indienne. Derrière nous, Jorge guidait les mulets, et nous froissions du genou avec un râpement morne, comme un gué interminable, le désert d'herbes peigné par le vent.

The Uplands of Sertalejo

To Jules Monnerot

I need only close my eyes for the memory of that faint season to return, when we roamed, Orlando and I, the uplands of Sertalejo. Once more I see the skies swept with the lustral clarity of a cleansed pebble shore, where the clouds sketched pearly shell-like spirals on the pure canvas—the green hills above the chasms, where the wind's fingers plunged into the tall grass—the mountain lakes, nestled in the heart of the star-shaped land serrated with peaks, like drops of night dew in the palm of a leaf. But above all, with the allure of a sustained chord that drowns out a melody's arabesques like still water, silence comes back to haunt me: a highland silence, of a devastated and smooth planet where nothing frays the clouds' shadows on the ground, and where sunlight bursts through the silent thunder of blooming life.

We made progress little by little, for in those plateaus fatigue can suddenly come over you like a lead coat over the shoulders, and the rarefied air of the high altitude made our hearts feverish. We started on the road in the early morning, when the air smelled like snow and stars and nipped at the belly—we folded up the tents and cleaned the guns. At first, we walked side by side, in good spirits from the morning's conversation, then the overgrowth along the path, a narrow rocky pass, separated us—words became fewer and farther between—and silence fell over our meager single-file line. Behind us, Jorge led the mules, and with a dull rustle, our knees would brush against the desert of wind-combed grass extending before us like an endless ford.

Nous traversions souvent d'immenses étendues de cette herbe sèche et craquante, couleur de paille, qu'on appelle le pajonal — et nul désert de sable ne pourrait donner l'idée de la tristesse de cette prairie momifiée et morte, comme desséchée sur pied par un mal mystérieux. Le bleu du ciel sur cette mer de paille virait à une teinte d'orage, le crissement de faux des pieds dans les tiges sèches agaçait les dents de sa grêle menue. Ces jours-là, l'étape était plus silencieuse que de coutume, et nous allions, absorbés par le crépitement incessant de ce frêle bruit de mort, dans un malaise vague : il nous semblait parfois que nous foulions le scalp de la planète.

Nulle part peut-être la nature ne m'avait paru atteindre à une netteté de lignes, à une austérité aussi lunaire. À l'horizon, l'air acide décapait cruellement chaque ligne, l'aiguisait, lui donnait sur l'œil l'attaque mordante du fil d'un rasoir. Sur ces chaumes tristes ne vibrait pas même une buée tremblante de chaleur. Nous marchions, le souffle court, les yeux meurtris, la bouche sèche, jusqu'à ce que devant nous un sillage brusque étoilât les herbes, et qu'un coup de feu brisât en miettes pour une minute le piège de cristal qui nous serrait les tempes de son gel.

En croisant sur ces hautes surfaces, parfois nous voyions venir à nous des montagnes. C'étaient toujours de ces grands volcans, aux lignes nobles, qui portent leur couronne avec une majesté solitaire de rois pasteurs sur les hautes steppes des Cordillères. Ils s'annonçaient d'habitude au crépuscule, sous l'aspect d'un nuage blanc en forme de cône ancré au-dessus de l'horizon dans la brume violette. Le matin les suspendait sur l'horizon, collés au ciel d'une ventouse de neige plus incandescente que de la lave, liés seulement à la terre par un double cil d'ombre d'une ligne pure, à peine distinct encore des bancs de brouillard — pareils, sur le haut lieu de cette immense table, au geste symétrique et solennel des bras dans l'ostension. Puis, à mesure que nous fendions les herbes, l'apparition dérivait sur l'horizon plat selon une orbe d'astre, avivant

We often crossed huge stretches of that dry and crisp grass, the color of straw, which they called *pajonal*—and no sand desert could hint at the desolation of that grassland, dead and mummified, left to dry out as if stricken by a mysterious illness. The sky's blue on that sea of straw turned into a storm's tint, the chattering teeth of its light hail disturbed by our feet crunching in the dry stalks like a scythe. Those days we were quieter than usual, and we fell, unsettled by the constant crackling of that fragile sound of death, into a faint unease: sometimes it felt as though we were treading on the planet's scalp.

It seemed to me that nowhere else in nature had achieved such a precision of line, so moonlike a barrenness. On the horizon, the stinging air cruelly stripped each line bare, sharpened it, gave it the biting menace of a razor's edge. Above those sad straw fields, not even a vapor of warmth quivered in the air. We walked short of breath, eyes bruised and mouths dry, until suddenly we saw footprints sprinkled in the grasses, and a gunshot momentarily shattered the crystal trap of frost that tightened our temples.

Crossing those high grounds, we sometimes saw mountains coming toward us. It was always those large volcanos, with noble lines, that wear their crowns with the solitary majesty of shepherd kings on the high steppes of the Cordilleras. They usually presented themselves at dusk, posing as white, conical clouds moored in the purple mist above the horizon. The morning suspended them in the air, stuck to the sky by a suction cup of snow more incandescent than lava and tied to the ground by their pure lines' lash-like shadows, scarcely distinct from the blankets of fog—the mountains, at the high place of that immense table, were like the symmetrical and ceremonious movement of gesticulating arms. As we chopped through the grasses, the apparition drifted over the flat horizon, following an orb of stars and brightening in its wake

successivement tous les coins du ciel — comme une blessure où la vie se fait plus attentive — d'un épiderme d'ange que le soir empourprait de fusées de rougeurs. L'apparition s'effaçait, et il se faisait ce plus profond silence que le ciel de nuit connaît après le passage d'une comète.

Par les nuits de ces grands pâturages, nous sentions les poumons dans notre poitrine jouer comme une bête qui s'éveille d'aise, élastique et fine, à l'épiderme subtil. Le vent du soir dans les hautes herbes balayait de la terre la dernière trace de moiteur, l'offrait au ciel nocturne dans la fraîcheur d'une grève lavée des mers froides. Nous recherchions d'instinct pour le campement du soir l'emplacement d'un tertre bas ; la flamme avivée par le vent faisait courir au loin une moire de cercles sur le luisant de l'herbe. Nous demeurions là longtemps, assis près du feu, surpris de cette lueur à l'horizon qui ne voulait pas mourir au-dessus des touffes noires. Le froid tombait : Jorge passait son poncho et s'éloignait vers les mules. Enfoui jusqu'au rebord de son manteau dans les herbes, il oscillait bizarrement à contre-jour sur la surface comme une statue portée sur un brancard. Une inquiétude exaltante prolongeait la veillée : sur ces plaines battantes comme une mer, le campement nous pesait comme l'ancre à un navire — comme par un soir de lune de détacher une barque, l'envie nous prenait de dériver, de nous laisser glisser dans les ténèbres extérieures comme dans un lit ouvert, odorant et plus secret. Orlando s'endormait : je me coulais dans les herbes, lissant du dos de la main les tiges déjà glacées, jusqu'à l'endroit éloigné où Jorge veillait près des mules, et je trouvais au fond de cette nuit deux yeux ouverts, comme le feu et la soupe chaude au bout d'une étape lointaine. Le feu mourait : avant le matin un peu de braise rose était le point le plus vivant de ces hautes terres, jusqu'à l'extrême horizon.

Il y a un allégement pour le cœur qui s'abandonne au pur voyage, et pour l'âme en migration, ne fût-ce que pour une

every corner of the sky with an angelic membrane—like life tending to a wound—which the evening made purple with bursts of red. The apparition faded, and in came a deeper silence, known to the night sky after a comet has passed.

On nights in those large pastures, we felt our lungs move in our chests like an animal waking at ease, supple and light, with delicate skin. The evening wind in the tall grasses swept the last traces of moisture from the ground, offering them to the night sky in the freshness of pebble shores cleansed by frigid seas. We searched instinctively for a spot on a low mound to set up camp; the flame kindled by the wind released circles of sparks into the distance over the gleaming grass. We stayed there a long while, sitting near the fire, surprised by that ever-present glow on the horizon above the black tufts. It was getting cold: Jorge put on his poncho and drew away toward the mules. Buried in the grasses up to the hem of his coat, he swayed strangely in the backlight, rising above the surface like a statue carried in a procession. An absorbing disquiet prolonged the vigil: on those plains beating like a sea, the camp weighed us down as an anchor does a ship—as on a moonlit evening one might be moved to untie a boat, we were taken by the urge to drift, to let ourselves glide through the outer darkness, to slip into a boundless, fragrant, and more secluded bed. Orlando was falling asleep: I stole away into the grasses, stroking the already frosty stalks with the back of my hand, and went up to the far-off spot where Jorge kept watch near the mules, and I found two open eyes in the depths of the night, like fire and warm soup at the end of a distant time to come. The fire was dying: a flicker of pink ember became the brightest point before dawn in those uplands, as far as the horizon.

There is comfort for the heart that gives way to pure voyage, and for the soul in migration, if only for a brief season, far from men's houses, an occasion for flight, a freshness of

saison brève, loin des maisons des hommes, un événement d'ailes, une fraîcheur de résurrection. Dans ces nuits où le froid prenait possession de la terre comme un nouveau règne, mon cœur se repaissait de sa force. Étendu de mon long sur ce toit du monde, les paumes ouvertes sur l'herbe glacée, mes yeux se diluaient comme une encre aux profondeurs clémentes du ciel nocturne, le gonflement de ma poitrine déferlait comme une marée à l'approfondissement infini des espaces, mon regard brûlait dans l'air pur comme le pur regard sans but d'une vigie, l'écorce fendue des pierres en livrait le froid vivant jusqu'à mon cœur. Au cœur de la nuit dissolvante, toutes amarres rompues, toute pesanteur larguée, docile au souffle et porté sur de l'eau, j'étais un lieu pur d'échange et d'alliance. À demi endormi déjà, dans l'excès de mon contentement, je serrais dans mes doigts la main de Jorge, en signe d'adieu et en signe de nouvel avènement.

revival. On those nights when the cold took possession of the earth, my heart reveled in its strength. I lay on the roof of the earth, palms open on the frosty grass, my eyes vanishing like an ink into the balmy depths of the night sky, the heaving of my chest breaking like a tide into the infinitely deepening ether, my gaze burning in the pure air like the pure, wandering gaze of a lookout, my heart pierced by the biting cold that was freed from the cracked stones. At the heart of the dissolving night, all cables cut, all weights cast off, surrendering to the air and carried on water, I was a pure vessel of exchange and communion. Already half asleep, in the excess of my contentment, I squeezed Jorge's hand in my fingers, as a sign of farewell and of a new coming.

La Sieste en Flandre hollandaise

À Mme S.L.

Au bord de l'Escaut oriental jusqu'à la banlieue d'Anvers, la Flandre hollandaise allonge une sorte de désert cultivé, une lisière habitable où la vie florale et grasse des bas pays semble se faire plus discrète qu'ailleurs. On n'y va, et on ne le traverse guère. Le pays se relie mal à la Zélande par quelques lignes de bacs qui traversent l'Escaut — du côté de la Belgique, au long des petites routes pavées, surgit très vite la silhouette d'un poste de douane, fleuri et endormi comme un chalet de ville d'eaux à la saison morte, où des douaniers hollandais flambant neuf dans leurs uniformes de *surplus* de la Royal Air Force somnolent dans une pièce ombragée et dévisagent avec une curiosité sans fièvre le touriste qui s'aventure dans ces solitudes excentriques. On bavarde sans hâte sous les arbres et dans la pièce minuscule comme dans le bureau d'octroi d'une petite ville, et on devine que les douaniers connaissent tout leur monde, car quiconque passe ici la frontière : journaliers hollandais qui vont travailler à Bruges, ou patrons belges du pilotage d'Anvers qui rejoignent Flessingue, ne saurait en général aller guère plus loin. La frontière passée, la sensation intime qui nous renseigne, en l'absence même de tout repère visible, sur les approches d'un lieu à l'écart s'insinue très vite dans l'esprit du voyageur. Il faut pénétrer là au crépuscule, quand les douaniers de l'équipe de jour rejoignent tout près de là leurs maisonnettes-jouets de briques rouges, pédalant tout droits sur leurs bicyclettes à long col de cygne, et que derrière soi les lignes verticales des clochers et des tours de Bruges, pareilles sur ces plaines basses au *skyline* lointain d'une ville d'Amérique, commencent à bleuir aux créneaux des files de peupliers. Les

Siesta in Dutch Flanders

To Madame S.L.

Along the banks of the Eastern Scheldt up to the outskirts
of Antwerp, Dutch Flanders extends a kind of cultivated des-
ert, a habitable forest edge where the floral and lush life of
the lowlands seems more hidden than anywhere else. No one
goes there, and almost no one crosses the land. The country
is poorly connected to Zeeland by a few ferry lines that cross
the Scheldt—on the Belgian side, along the small paved roads,
there suddenly emerges the silhouette of a customs post, cov-
ered in flowers and sleeping like a spa-town chalet in the off
season, where Dutch officers, newly minted in their *surplus*
uniforms of the Royal Air Force, doze in a shaded room and,
with a dull curiosity, stare at the tourist who ventures into
those outlying solitudes. We talk leisurely under the trees and
in the tiny room as though in a small town's tax office, and we
guess that the customs officers know everyone in their world,
for whoever crosses the border here—Dutch day laborers
going to work in Bruges, or Belgian captains of the Antwerp
boat service making their way to Flushing—generally can't go
much further. The border once crossed, the inner sense that
informs us, in the absence of any visible indication, of an ap-
proaching place *in the distance* soon creeps into the traveler's
spirit. The country should be entered at twilight, when the day
team's officers return to their little red brick houses nearby,
pedaling straight ahead on their gooseneck bicycles, and when
the vertical lines of Bruges's steeples and towers in the back-
ground, like the distant *skyline* of an American city on those
low plains, begin to turn blue in the gaps between the rows
of poplars. The empty roads seem to lose their blood little by

routes vides semblent perdre leur sang peu à peu en courant vers le nord, s'étoilent et s'étiolent en chemins plus petits qui fuient indéfiniment derrière leurs lignes d'arbres au travers du désert verdoyant. Aucun toit ne pointe plus derrière les masses des arbres, et aucune lumière ne brille encore. Le soir s'emplit d'une odeur d'herbe et de feuilles juteuses, aussi submergeante que celle d'une bête mouillée ; les troupeaux couchés dans le lointain déjà brumeux des grandes prairies semblent pris dans les remous figés de l'herbe haute comme dans la glu d'une banquise molle ; l'impression se fait jour que la vie, empêtrée dans cette verdure féroce, va s'engourdir là, finir, un peu plus loin : derrière ce rideau de peupliers. Il fait bon rouler dans la fraîcheur du soir sur ces routes touffues et sourdes, dont on arrive très vite à douter qu'elles mènent nulle part, zigzaguant sur la crête des digues entre les caissons titanesques des polders que le soir égalise, et qui se succèdent dans leur symétrie monotone comme d'immenses bacs où se décanterait pesamment une eau grasse sous sa moquette crémeuse d'écume verte. La végétation perd ici le caractère fantasque et inégal qu'on lui voit dans les pays vallonnés : elle *monte* plutôt, sur le fond plat des cases de ce damier énorme — égale, vorace, submergeante, étale — comme le niveau de la mer dans un bassin de marée, ou plutôt comme dans une rizière qu'on inonde, et où le tapis serré de pousses vertes qui lutte de vitesse avec l'eau semble se soulever comme une croûte flottante. Il n'y a pas de couture à cette robe verte — pas de lacune à ce revêtement pelucheux et universel : les pavés inégaux des routes suintent d'herbe juteuse, et le sommet même des digues est un tapis ondulant et silencieux où le sillage isolé d'un cycliste se referme comme la passée d'un doigt dans une fourrure. Pourtant la route continue, toujours plus rétrécie et plus inégale — une dernière courbe, et un raidillon minuscule escalade une digue qui fermait la vue : pour l'instant la lèpre verte n'a pas mangé plus loin et on voit l'Escaut, large et gris,

little the farther north they go, splitting and withering into smaller paths that flee indefinitely behind the lines of trees through the verdant desert. No roofs rise behind the trees any longer, and no lights still shine. The evening fills with a smell of grass and luscious leaves, overpowering as the odor of a wet animal; the herds lying in the large meadows already hazy in the distance seem entangled in the frozen swirls of the tall grass as though in the birdlime of a soft ice floe; the impression emerges that life, bogged down in this savage greenery, will go numb here, will end, a bit farther down: behind this curtain of poplars. It's pleasant to drive in the evening freshness, along these lush and muted roads, which we quickly come to suspect lead nowhere, zigzagging along the dikes' peaks between the polders' colossal coffers that the evening levels out and which succeed each other in their monotonous symmetry, like huge vats in which a kind of lush water might be decanted beneath its creamy carpet of green foam. Here, the vegetation loses the whimsical and patchy character seen in rolling countries: rather, it *rises*, onto the flat square surfaces of this enormous checkerboard—level, voracious, engulfing, motionless—like the sea level in a tidal basin or perhaps in a flooded rice field, and where a taut rug of green shoots that races the water seems to rise like a floating crust. There are no seams in this green dress—no holes in this plush and widespread covering: juicy grass seeps through the roads' uneven cobbles, and the very peaks of the dikes are silent and rippling rugs where a cyclist's secluded trail disappears, like a finger pressing into a fur coat. Yet the road goes on, always shrinking and becoming more uneven—a final curve, and a tiny steep path scales a dike that obstructed our view: for the moment, the green leprosy has eaten no further into the land and we see the Scheldt at low tide, vast and gray, reluctantly revealing the large vulnerable puddles of its mudflats' naked skin, where the high tide left teeth marks and the grass grabs and clings

découvrant à regret à marée basse aux morsures de son ad-
versaire les grandes flaques vulnérables de peau nue de ses
vasières où l'herbe croche et s'agrippe. Les fumées des cargos
qui remontent à Anvers défilent avec une insolence paresseuse
entre les cuirassements hostiles de ces berges vautrées dans
une somnolence lourde et agricole — sitôt leur revers dévalé,
on ne voit plus rien; pourtant on s'avise alors de la proximité
du large au souffle plus vif qui lave ces campagnes amples et
aérées, à leurs ciels changeants et rapides qui font courir l'om-
bre des nuages sur les lacs d'herbe, et aux rappels des oiseaux
de mer dont tournoient un moment par-dessus les peupliers
les nuées criardes, avant de regagner les vasières pour la nuit.
Le point de vue change : un instant, pour l'œil prévenu, sur
cet océan colmaté des prairies, les voilures serrées des peu-
pliers reprennent la fuite perspective et noble des escadres
de ligne sous leurs tours de toile, telles qu'on les voit dans
les vieux tableaux hollandais d'histoire, au rez-de-chaussée du
Rijksmuseum.

Tout ce pays, très récemment endigué, vient de sortir de
l'eau, c'est visible, dans l'éclatement floral d'un lendemain de
déluge. Pourtant le vide et le silence de ces campagnes ex-
ubérantes intriguent. On dirait que la vie s'intimide devant
cette étoffe neuve et roide taillée à lés trop réguliers et trop
amples, s'accroche mal à ce parcellement dépaysant de cyclope.
Elle chemine agrippée aux digues, comme un insecte en suiv-
ant les raies du plancher, envahit précautionneusement par
les bandes cet éden de verdure préfabriqué dont la géométrie
distendue et austère la désoriente : on dirait qu'une espèce
d'*agoraphobie* la refoule d'instinct vers les bordures ombragées
des grands viviers d'herbes. Il n'y a pas de villes et guère de
villages : l'homme s'est découragé de préférer un lieu à un
autre dans la juxtaposition sans nervures de ce carrelage ag-
ricole ; sa prise s'affermit d'abord dans les angles, à la façon
des toiles d'araignée colonisant une maison neuve. Parfois

to the ground. The fumes of cargo ships returning to Antwerp pass with a lazy insolence between the hostile armor-plating of those banks lolling in a heavy and rustic drowsiness—the last of the fumes once gone, we see nothing; yet we're reminded of the sea's proximity thanks to the brisk wind that cleanses this wide, airy countryside, the changing, swift skies that make clouds' shadows pass over lakes of grass, the calls of seabirds whose screeching flocks swirl momentarily above the poplars, before returning to the mudflats for the night. Our point of view shifts: now, for the predisposed eye, on this ocean filled with meadows, the poplars' taut sails flee toward the noble vanishing point like the canvas towers of lined-up squadrons, as can be seen in old Dutch history paintings on the ground floor of the Rijksmuseum.

This entire country, recently diked, has just emerged from water, in the floral explosion of the aftermath of a flood. Yet this exuberant land is curious in its emptiness and silence. Life seems intimidated before this new and stiff fabric trimmed to widths too even and too long, and poorly hangs on to this unsettling division of cycloptic plots. It makes its way clinging to the dikes, like an insect following the cracks on a floor, it passes cautiously through the strips of land, invading this manufactured Eden of greenery and disoriented by its distended and stark geometry: a kind of *agoraphobia* seems to instinctively push it outward to the shaded edges of the large fish ponds of grasses. There are no towns and scarcely any villages: the juxtaposition of these ribless agricultural tiles discouraged man from preferring one place to the other; his hold on them was first established in the corners, like cobwebs colonizing a new house. Sometimes a tiny village leans into the acute angle formed by two dikes: it can hardly be seen unless approached from above; the small houses' roofs are just level with the dike: the eye plunges over the flower-lined window-sills and into the narrow, frighteningly clean rooms with tiled

un village minuscule s'accote ainsi dans l'angle aigu de deux digues : on ne le voit guère qu'en arrivant dessus ; les toits des maisonnettes-jouets affleurent tout juste au niveau de la digue : l'œil plonge sur les accotements fleuris des fenêtres et dans les menues pièces carrelées, d'une propreté effrayante, et l'on voit le départ des raides petits escaliers de guillotine. Il n'y a personne, les jardinets sont vides, le village est si petit qu'on le tiendrait dans la main, il se chauffe là, tout coi, bercé dans le soleil pâle, étalant sans gêne aux yeux son menu *far-niente* domestique, comme les hamacs de l'équipage sous les panneaux ouverts du poste d'avant. L'opulence s'est réfugiée dans les grandes fermes neuves et correctes aux briques lui-santes : quelquefois, après avoir zigzagué jusqu'à la lassitude aux angles droits de ces cases béantes et pourtant si apparem-ment *destinées*, du haut d'une digue soudain on en découvre une, et on éprouve un petit tressaillement intime à constater que l'alvéole, cette fois, est habitée, mais aucun chemin ne ray-onne d'elle, aucune éraflure à l'entour ne griffe le tapis vert immaculé, nul de ces liens ténus que tisse le long ménage des champs ne l'arrime au paysage — simplement elle est posée là, un signe épuré et curieusement abstrait de l'occupation plutôt que de la présence, indifférente et amovible comme une pièce sur la case d'un échiquier. Il n'y a pas d'allées et venues autour des bâtisses muettes, et pas même de chant de coq dans leur cour : sous leurs toits qui chevauchent les pi-gnons jusqu'à terre, comme la fourche d'un cavalier distendue par un ventre énorme, elles ont la rumination pesante d'un *souffleur* enfoui jusqu'aux narines dans le plancton ou d'un troupeau vautré dans l'après-midi de la Prairie; leurs noms mêmes : Baarn, Graauw, Saaftingen, semblent bâiller en leur milieu sur leur double voyelle traînante comme sur un mu-gissement paresseux et bucolique. Pourtant on se laisse aller à s'imaginer pleine de charme la vie de ces fermes cossues et rebondies, aux doux flancs farcis d'herbe engrangée — un

flooring and catches a glimpse of the foot of stairs, small and steep like those of a guillotine. No one's around, the little gardens are empty, the village is so small that it could be held in one's hand, snuggled up, calm, cradled in the pale sun, shamelessly displaying its domestic *farniente* before our eyes, like the officers' hammocks under the outpost's open signs. Opulence took refuge in the large, well-built farms new with gleaming bricks: sometimes, after tiring of zigzagging along the right angles of those expansive yet so apparently *determined* squares, from the top of a dike suddenly we come upon one of them, then shudder slightly to find that this time the cell is inhabited, but no paths radiate from it, no surrounding abrasion scratches the immaculate green rug, none of those thin threads woven by the cultivation of fields attach it to the landscape— it simply sits there, a stripped and curiously abstract sign of occupation rather than a presence, indifferent and removable like a chess piece on the square of a board. There are no comings and goings around the mute buildings, and not even a cock's crow in their yards: under their roofs that sit astride gables low as the ground, like a horse rider's forked legs distended by an enormous belly, the buildings bear the weighty rumination of a *dolphin* buried up to its nostrils in plankton or of a sprawled-out herd in the Meadow's afternoon; their very names: Baarn, Graauw, Saaftinge, seem to yawn midway with the drawl of their double vowels, as though in an idle and bucolic bellow. Yet we let ourselves imagine the life of those prosperous, robust farms, full of charm, with sweet slopes plump with gathered grass—a charm formed by forgetfulness and a subtle burial beneath the unsettling anonymity of their identical constructions: perhaps no place in the world that gives one so indifferent a feeling of living *somewhere*—somewhere lost in the savanna's welcoming plots of houses, in the cultivated sea of grasses, walled in at the heart of the unmarked labyrinth of the poplars' screen a thousand times folded and doubled onto

charme fait d'oubli et d'ensevelissement plus subtil derrière l'anonymat déroutant de leurs bâtisses pareilles : aucun lieu du monde peut-être où l'on doive se sentir aussi indifféremment vivre *quelque part* — quelque part perdu dans le lotissement hospitalier de savane, dans le large aménagé des herbes, muré au cœur du labyrinthe sans repères de l'écran mille fois replié et redoublé sur lui-même des peupliers. Le désert a ses perspectives où l'imagination s'engouffre, la forêt la vie cachée de sa pénombre et de ses bruits — ici la sensation intime qu'on s'est perdu, pour être sans fièvre, se fait plus subtile et plus absorbante. On peut cheminer pendant des heures d'une case à l'autre de cet immense jeu de l'oie, dans le bruissement obsédant des peupliers et l'odeur d'herbe écrasée, jamais la vue ne va plus loin que la prochaine digue et le prochain rideau d'arbres ; du fond plat de chacune des alvéoles, nul ne voit et nul n'est vu ; derrière la première digue s'allonge une digue pareille, et derrière l'écran des arbres un autre rideau de peupliers. Nulle angoisse dans ce labyrinthe impeccable et soigné, au vert profond de pelouse anglaise : l'homme est là tout près, et les routes carrossables ; il suffirait de faire un signe, mais c'est l'envie de faire ce signe qui manque, et on s'aperçoit que le besoin cesserait très vite, pris dans le dédale obsédant des chambres de verdure, de s'orienter vers aucun point de ralliement. L'idée tout à coup vous traverse qu'on pourrait s'étendre là, ne plus penser à rien, enfoui dans le manteau épais et l'odeur de feuilles fraîches, le visage lavé par le vent léger, le bruissement doux et perpétuel des peupliers dans les oreilles vous apprivoisant à la rumeur même de la plénitude. Une certaine *base*, essentielle à la vie, précipite seulement dans cet immense volume de calme. Tout est soudain très loin, les contours de toute pensée se dissolvent dans la brume verte, la dernière chambre du labyrinthe donne sur une disposition intime de l'âme où l'on craint de regarder : la fleur mystérieuse qu'elle abrite, c'est à la plante humaine qu'il

itself. The desert has its views that engulf the imagination, the forest, the hidden life of its half-light and sounds—here the intimate feeling of having lost one's way, so as to free oneself from all agitation, is made subtler and more absorbing. We can spend hours making our way from one square to the other in this huge goose game, in the haunting rustle of poplars and the smell of trampled grass, the view never goes past the next dike or curtain of trees; from the flat base of each cell, no one sees and no one is seen; behind the first dike extends another identical dike, and behind the screen of trees, another curtain of poplars. No anxiety in this impeccable and spotless labyrinth, in the deep green of an English lawn: man is right there, and the roads are drivable; it'd be enough to wave a hand, but the desire to wave is missing, and we realize that, caught in the haunting maze of these chambers of greenery, the need to head toward any rallying point would quickly cease. Suddenly the idea crosses your mind that we might rest there and think of nothing more, buried in the thick mantle and smell of fresh leaves, your face cleansed by the light wind, the gentle and perpetual rustle of poplars in your ears subduing you to the very murmur of plenitude. A certain *basis*, essential to life, precipitates only in this immense sound of calm. Everything is suddenly very far, the contours of every thought dissolve in green haze, the labyrinth's final chamber leads to an intimate disposition of the soul where we're afraid to look: the mysterious flower it shelters—this is what the human plant is asked to unfold in a euphoria of concord with the deep spirits of Indifference. We lie down and give way to the grass. Thought evacuates its wearisome watchtowers and shuts down the network of its useless outposts; it flows from every direction to the threshold of the pure consciousness of being; at the body's frontiers, it is now nothing more than a light perspiration whose purpose seems only to refresh us by evaporating, releasing into the void an overflow

est demandé de la faire s'entrouvrir dans une ivresse d'acqui-
escement aux esprits profonds de l'Indifférence. On cède de
tout son long à l'herbe. La pensée évacue ses postes de guet
fastidieux et replie le réseau de ses antennes inutiles ; elle re-
flue de toutes parts vers la ligne d'arrêt de la pure conscience
d'être ; elle n'est plus aux frontières du corps qu'une légère
sueur qui ne semble faite que pour nous rafraîchir en s'évapo-
rant à mesure, dissiper dans le néant un trop-plein de sève qui
monte, dans l'épaisse sécrétion végétale, de l'apoplexie de cette
nature verte et de cette argile qui se souvient intimement de
la mer. Le monde reflue sur nous compact dans le retrait des
pointes acérées de l'interrogation qui le dilacère ; le corps qui
fait fléchir sous l'herbe la vase encore molle ne se sent plus
fait que pour prêter à la respiration vorace qui le soulève le
sentiment d'une liberté fonctionnelle encore inconnue : on
dirait que les pores de la terre sont ici plus ouverts qu'ailleurs.
Plus d'horizon, mais plutôt l'opacité immatérielle d'un voile
de tulle qu'approche de ce sommeil éveillé comme une mous-
tiquaire une débauche sans mesure d'inattention : la contrac-
tion de cette fine bulle de transparence emprisonne autour
de nous sans mutilation un morceau indifférencié de nature
suffisante : rien de plus que ce froissement d'herbe frais sous
les paumes, le scintillement sur le ciel des feuilles de tremble
qui semble aiguiser l'immobilité, et dans ce *milieu* où toutes
les pressions s'annulent et s'équilibrent, un ludion désancré
qui flotte jusqu'à la nausée entre l'herbe et les nuages. Ce mo-
ment, et ce lieu exigu de la terre, tient en nous sa totalité
et sa suffisance — il n'y a plus d'ailleurs — il n'y a jamais eu
d'ailleurs — toutes choses communient parfaitement dans le
perméable ; on se sent là, aux lisières attirantes de l'absorption,
une goutte entre les gouttes, exprimée un moment avant d'y
rentrer de l'éponge molle de la terre.

of sap rising in a thick vegetal secretion from the apoplexy of this green nature and clay that intimately recalls the sea. The world flows over us, resistant to the retreating sharp tips of the question that tears it to pieces; the body that makes the soft earth dip under the grass is felt to exist only to lend the intense breathing, which raises it, the feeling of a functional freedom as of yet unknown: here the earth's pores seem open wider than anywhere else. No longer a horizon, but rather a tulle veil's immaterial opacity brought near this waking sleep by an immense orgy of thoughtlessness like a mosquito net: around us, the contraction of this fine, transparent bubble imprisons, without mutilating, an undistinguished piece of earth sufficient in itself: nothing more than this crumpling of fresh grass under palms, in the sky the twinkling of aspen leaves that seems to sharpen the stillness, and in this *milieu* where all pressures cancel and balance out, an unanchored Cartesian diver floating to the point of nausea between the grass and clouds. This moment, and this confined place on earth, holds its totality and sufficiency within us—elsewhere no longer exists—elsewhere never did exist—all things are perfectly as one in the permeable; we feel ourselves there, at the alluring edges of absorption, a drop among drops, revealed for a moment before receding into the soft sponge of the earth.

Gomorrhe

En ce temps-là — c'était les jours les plus longs de l'année — à travers les halliers du Cinglais de grands chars de combat tenaient l'affût au coude des laies forestières, la volée de leurs pièces charbonnée contre le soleil couchant des châteaux Louis XIII. La lumière était désheurée — l'ombre des buissons au travers de la route plus délectable que l'eau fraîche, à cause de ces mouches de fer brillantes et du remue-ménage dans le ciel de mauvais guêpier. C'était d'aller à l'air libre qui plaisait : le large des routes, les portes battantes — à même la pelouse d'herbe surie dans la gentilhommière évacuée le camp volant sous les platanes, au large de la ville irrespirable. De grosses gouttes d'orage tombaient dans les plats ; par les doubles fenêtres ouvertes, on voyait les lits de camp d'enfants sous les portraits de famille, dans un salon plus déployé qu'une charge de cavalerie. L'Orne coulait devant — très lente — parmi les troènes et les prairies de fleurs pleines de joncs. Cela me plaisait que la vie fût ainsi desserrée, et qu'on fît sa couchée dans les maisons vagues comme au fond d'un bois noir.

Quand j'arrivai à la côte de May, le versant était mi-parti d'ombre et de soleil ; les oiseaux chantaient moins fort ; une jeune fille que je connaissais allait devant moi sur la route très blanche : je la rejoignis. Je compris que son étape aussi était à Jaur et qu'invités, nous devions coucher dans la même maison. Nous allâmes. C'était une contrée charmante : ces côtes qui montaient entre des forêts, la fraîcheur des feuilles et les bas-côtés d'argile humide qui gardent des flaques jusqu'au cœur de l'été. Quelquefois nous parlions et quelquefois nous nous taisions. Il y avait des bouquets de sapins noirs plantés à l'embranchement des routes, ou parfois un calvaire — mais le plus

Gomorrah

In those days—the longest of the year—across the thickets of
the Forest of Cinglais, great tanks kept a lookout at the bends
in the dirt paths, their projectiles leaving charcoal trails against
the setting sun of Louis XIII châteaux. The light was running
late—the bushes' shade on the road more delectable than fresh
water, owing to those shining iron flies and the commotion of
a vicious swarm in the sky. It was pleasing to saunter out into
the open air: the expanse of roads, the swinging doors—the
camp-volant under the plane trees, on the lawn of withered
grass in the evacuated manor, distant from the stifling town.
Large storm drops fell into dishes; through the open double
windows, one could see children's cots under family portraits,
in a room better arranged than a cavalry charge. The Orne
flowed ahead—very slowly—among the privets and meadows
full of flowers and bulrushes. I liked that life was loose in its
way, and that nights were spent in remote houses as though
deep in a black wood.

When I arrived at the hill in May-sur-Orne, the slope was
half in shade and half in sun; the birds were singing more
softly; a young girl I knew was walking ahead of me onto the
white road: I joined her. I understood that she was also stop-
ping off at Jaur and that, as guests, we'd be passing the night in
the same house. We made our way along. It was a charming re-
gion: those hills that rose between forests, the fresh leaves and
the humid clay roadsides that retained their puddles until the
height of summer. At times we talked, at times we fell silent.
There were clusters of black firs planted at the junctions, or
now and then a calvary—but loveliest of all was that summer
evening which kept the fields awake so late, supernaturally

beau, c'était cette soirée d'été qui tenait les champs éveillés si tard, surnaturellement, comme les jours où l'on moissonne, à cause de l'*heure allemande*. À Thury, je m'arrêtai pour dîner à l'auberge : le soleil bas flambait encore aux carreaux et aux cuivres des armoires — je relevais les yeux entre les plats sur la route vide, qui coulait limpide et toute pure devant la porte ouverte, comme une rivière qu'on fait passer à travers son jardin. Je repartis tout éclairé par la chanson d'une bouteille de vin, comme une lanterne par sa bougie. Derrière moi, les sirènes l'une après l'autre amorçaient leur décrue sur la ville marquée pour le feu. Il n'y aurait plus à s'inquiéter jamais. La route devant était toute blanche de lune, si délicatement éclairée qu'on distinguait, sur les bas-côtés, les jeunes lames de l'herbe entre les graviers fins. Le clocher de Jaur flanquait le chemin à quelques jets de pierre, dans la nuit marquée d'un signe tendre, comme une robe blanche dans l'ombre d'un jardin — la route allait vers le Sud, toute sablée entre les tentes des pommiers ronds dans la nuit ouverte, et je chantais parce que j'étais attendu.

so as on harvest days, because of the *German hour*. At Thury, I stopped at an inn for dinner: the low sun was still gleaming on the windowpanes and the cabinets' copper hinges—I looked up between courses at the empty road, which flowed limpid and pure before the open door, like a river one lets pass through the garden. I left, glowing from the song of a bottle of wine, like a lantern lit by a candle. Behind me, sirens one after another began their descent into the town bound for fire. There'd be nothing to worry about ever again. The road ahead was white with moonlight, so delicately lit that one could make out, on the roadsides, new blades of grass between the fine gravel. The bell tower of Jaur adjoined the path a few stone's throws away, in the night marked by a tender sign, like a white dress in a garden's shadow—the road went toward the South, covered with sand among the tents of round apple trees in the open night, and I sang because someone was expecting me.

Aubrac

Il faut si peu pour vivre ici. De ce balcon où penche la montagne à l'heure où le soleil est plus jaune, il ne reste plus à choisir qu'à droite la banquette où l'herbe noircit sous les châtaigniers, à gauche la Viadène au loin déjà toute bleue. À mi-pente, la journée respire. De cette galerie ample et couverte où glisse la route de gravier rose au-dessus du Causse gris-perdrix, on voit mûrir très bas les ombres longues dans la lumière couleur de prune. Tout commande de faire halte à ce reposoir encore tempéré où la terre penche, pour respirer l'air luxueux de parc arrosé, la journée qui s'engrange dans les rais du miel et la chaleur de l'ambre, jusqu'à ce que l'œil gorgé revienne à la route rose qui monte sous le soleil avant de tourner dans l'ombre d'un bois de sapins, et que ta main déjà fraîchisse avec le soir — ta main qui laisse filtrer le bruit plus clair du torrent, ta main qui me tend les colchiques de l'automne.

Nous monterons plus haut. Là où plus haut que tous les arbres, la terre nappée de basalte hausse et déplisse dans l'air bleu une paume immensément vide, à l'heure plus froide où tes pieds nus s'enfonceront dans la fourrure respirante, où tes cheveux secoueront dans le vent criblé d'étoiles l'odeur du foin sauvage, pendant que nous marcherons ainsi que sur la mer vers le phare de lave noire par la terre nue comme une jument.

Aubrac

One needs so little to live here. From this balcony where the mountain leans at the hour of the yellowing sun, one has only to choose the bench to the right where the grass darkens under the chestnut trees, Viadène to the left already blue in the distance. Halfway up the hill, the day breathes. From this wide and covered gallery where the rosy gravel road glides above the partridge-gray Causses, long shadows can be seen below, maturing in the plum-colored light. Everything asks that you pause, at this still-temperate resting place where the earth tilts, to breathe the luscious air of the dewy park, the day that takes refuge in honey rays and amber warmth, until the saturated eye returns to the rosy road that rises under the sun before turning into a pine forest's shade, and until your hand has already cooled with the evening—your hand that filters the torrent's sharp sound, your hand that offers me autumn crocuses.

We'll go higher still. Higher than all the trees, where the earth glazed with basalt raises and unfolds an immensely empty palm in the blue air, at a colder hour when your bare feet will sink into the breathing carpet, when your hair will shake off the smell of wild hay in the wind riddled with stars, and all the while we'll walk as though on water toward the lighthouse of black lava, like a mare across the naked earth.

La Route

The Road

Ce fut, si je me souviens bien, dix jours après avoir franchi la Crête que nous atteignîmes l'entrée du Perré ; l'étroit chemin pavé qui conduisait sur des centaines de lieues de la lisière des Marches aux passes du Mont-Harbré — la dernière ligne de vie, vingt fois tronçonnée et ressoudée, qui joignait encore par intervalles le Royaume à la Montagne cernée et lointaine.

L'étrange — l'inquiétante route ! le seul *grand chemin* que je n'aie jamais suivi, dont le serpentement, quand bien même tout s'effacerait autour de lui de ses rencontres et de ses dangers — de ses taillis crépusculaires et de sa peur — creuserait encore sa trace dans ma mémoire comme un rai de diamant sur une vitre. On s'engageait dans celui-là comme on s'embarque sur la mer. À travers trois cents lieues de pays confus, courant seul, sans nœuds, sans attaches, un fil mince, étiré, blanchi de soleil, pourri de feuilles mortes, il déroule dans mon souvenir la traînée phosphorescente d'un sentier où le pied tâtonne entre les herbes par une nuit de lune, comme si, entre ses berges de nuit, je l'avais suivi d'un bout à l'autre à travers un interminable bois noir.

Il commençait bizarrement — à la manière de ces fragments de chaussée romaine qui commencent et finissent sans qu'on sache pourquoi au milieu d'un champ, comme une règle qu'on laisserait tomber sur un échiquier — au cœur même d'une clairière d'herbes, dans l'intervalle formé par deux lisières de forêts qui couraient se rejoindre, et entre lesquelles il s'engageait. Là où le soubassement en était resté intact, il présentait, quoiqu'il fût très étroit, tous les signes d'une construction soigneuse : une maçonnerie compacte de petits blocs anguleux, ou parfois, près du lit des rivières, de galets ronds,

It was, if I remember correctly, ten days after crossing the Peak that we reached the opening of the Embankment, the narrow-paved path that stretched hundreds of leagues from the edge of the Borderlands to the passes of Mount Harbré—the last lifeline, cut away and resoldered twenty times over, that still linked at intervals the Kingdom to the distant and surrounded Mountain.

The strange, unsettling road! The only *open road* I've ever taken, whose meandering would—even if everything around it were to fade away, from its perils and junctions to its fear and twilight thickets—still engrave its imprint in my memory, like the scratch of a diamond on a windowpane. Entering that path was like setting out to sea. Across 300 leagues of haphazard land, extending on its own, a thin thread disentangled and untied, drawn-out, bleached by the sun, and rotten with dead leaves, it unfurls, in my memory, the phosphorescent trail where feet feel their way through grass on a moonlit night, as though I had followed it along its nocturnal riverbanks, from one end to the other, across an endless black wood.

It began curiously—similar to the way those fragments of Roman roads begin and end in the middle of a field for no apparent reason, like a straight-edge dropped onto a chessboard—in the midst of a grassy clearing, in the space formed by the edges of two forests going around to meet each other. Where the base layers had stayed intact, the road, though very narrow, gave every indication of careful construction: a work of compact masonry made of little sharp-cut blocks—or sometimes, close to the riverbed, of round pebbles embedded in a sort of concrete—where a pavement had been leveled and

pris dans une sorte de béton, sur laquelle on avait aplani et rejointoyé un pavage de grosses dalles plates. L'ensemble figurait à peu près le sommet d'une étroite digue qui eût affleuré au niveau du sol. Sa résonance mate et sans vibration sous les pieds des chevaux était celle d'un mur. Bien que sa largeur atteignît tout juste la voie d'une charrette, et qu'il fût visible que le chemin avait dû être surtout un chemin cavalier, les dalles de la surface gardaient des traces anciennes d'ornières qui mordaient la roche d'une gouttière usée, incrustée maintenant de lichens gris, et ces signes d'un trafic ancien évoquaient de façon vive l'idée d'un courant ininterrompu, d'un éveil de vie qui avait dû, à une époque très reculée, animer la route de bout en bout. L'impression de délabrement extrême qu'elle donnait maintenant n'en était que plus forte. C'était une route fossile : la volonté qui avait sabré de cette estafilade les solitudes pour y faire affluer le sang et la sève était depuis longtemps morte — et mortes même les conditions qui avaient guidé cette volonté ; il restait une cicatrice blanchâtre et indurée, mangée peu à peu par la terre comme par une chair qui se reforme, dont la direction pourtant creusait encore l'horizon vaguement ; un signe engourdi, crépusculaire, d'aller plus avant plutôt qu'une voie — une ligne de vie usée qui végétait encore au travers des friches comme sur une paume. Elle était si ancienne que, depuis sa construction, la configuration même du terrain avait dû changer insensiblement : par endroits, le soubassement de la chaussée dominait maintenant d'assez haut en talus les prairies des vallées, montrant à nu tout un hérissonnage de blocs — ailleurs, le dallage submergé plongeait sur d'assez grandes distances et se perdait sous les terres rapportées. Pourtant on ne la quittait jamais tout à fait de vue, ou plutôt — même submergée sous les éboulis, plongée sous les hautes herbes — , comme le cheval tâte encore du sabot le fond empierré du gué, on gardait avec elle une espèce de contact singulier, car la trace d'un chemin

repointed with large flat slabs. The ensemble resembled the top of a narrow dike that had reached ground level. Its dull resonance, numb to the vibrations of horses' hooves, was like that of a wall. Though it barely spanned the width of a wagon-cart lane, and although it was clear that the path must have been mainly for horses, the slabs on the surface preserved ancient imprints of ruts biting into the rock, now encrusted with gray lichen, of a timeworn gutter, and these marks of past traffic vividly brought to mind the idea of a continuous current, of a dawning of life that, at some point far back in time, must have invigorated the road from end to end. It now gave an impression of extreme dilapidation that was all the stronger. The road was a fossil: the will that had made blood and sap flow into the solitudes cut from this gash had been dead for a long time—dead too were the circumstances that had guided this will; there remained an indurated, whitish scar—eaten bit by bit by the earth like a wound being healed by its flesh—whose direction was vaguely outlined still by the horizon, not a route but twilight's muted sign to go forward, a worn lifeline that continued to sprout across the wilderness, as it might across a palm. It was so old that, since its construction, the very configuration of the terrain must have gradually changed: in some places, the base layers were now raised in rather high slopes that overlooked the meadows of the valleys, exposing the blocks of rock; elsewhere, the submerged paving plunged into the ground over long distances, receding into the overturned earth. Yet the road was never fully out of sight, or rather, even when it was submerged under piles of fallen rocks, immersed in tall grass, one kept a special contact with it, like a horse feeling a ford's stony bottom against its hooves, for the remnants of a manmade road take longer to disappear from the earth than a scar left by a red-hot iron: from a hole in the bushes coming into sight, to some sudden, rigid alignment of trees in the distance, to any living indication of *direction*,

d'homme est plus longue à s'effacer de la terre que la marque d'un fer rouge : à une trouée plus claire devant soi dans les buissons, à je ne sais quel alignement soudain plus rigide des arbres dans l'éloignement, quelle suggestion encore vivante de *direction*, la Route, de loin en loin, désincarnée, continuait à nous faire signe, comme ces anges énigmatiques des chemins de la Bible qui, loin devant, du seul doigt levé faisaient signe de les suivre, sans daigner même se retourner. Elle ressemblait aux rivières des pays de sable qui cessent de couler à la saison chaude et se fragmentent en un chapelet de mares, entre lesquelles un filet d'eau gargouille parfois encore entre les cailloux ; depuis des âges lointains le sang avait cessé d'y battre de bout en bout, mais on devinait, à des passages marqués de traces plus fraîches de roues ou de sabots, que le sens une fois perdu et jusqu'à l'idée même du long voyage, le sommeil n'était pas descendu sur elle d'un seul coup : de façon discontinue, et sur des parcours de faible longueur, on avait continué à l'emprunter par endroits, comme un laboureur fait cahoter sa charrette sur un bout de voie romaine qui traverse son champ — mais c'était alors un charroi menu et tout à fait domestique, comme il en chemine dans les venelles des petits bourgs entre les meules et les abreuvoirs — troupeaux de petit bétail qu'on mène pâturer ou vendre, allées et venues de charbonniers ou de bûcherons, colporteurs qui se risquaient jusque-là de la lisière des Marches. Puis, à mesure qu'on s'enfonçait davantage dans les solitudes confuses, même ces petits craquements humains de chemin creux mouraient, et après le grand vide blanc de la journée, dans le chien et loup du crépuscule, c'étaient les bêtes libres qui prenaient là un dernier relai, car cette éclaircie dans les bois leur semblait familière et commode, surtout à celles qui voyagent et vont loin ; souvent on entendait derrière le proche tournant, le galop d'un harde sur les pierres, ou bien dans l'éloignement, avec des grognements d'aise, on voyait trotter dans le fil du chemin, d'un long

the Road, disembodied, continued to beckon us from time to time, like those enigmatic angels in the Bible, who far ahead would signal men to follow them simply by raising a finger, without even deigning to look back. It resembled the rivers that flow through desert land and dry out in the summer heat, and which break into a string of ponds, where a trickle of water sometimes gurgles once more among the stones; for ages, the blood had ceased beating from end to end, but one could guess from a few crossings marked by fresher wheel tracks or hoof prints that, once the meaning and very idea of a long journey was lost, sleep had not seized it in one go: unevenly and over short distances, people had passed across the road in certain places—like a plowman who rattles his cart over a section of a Roman road that cuts through his field, but it must have been a small wagon, no doubt for domestic purposes, like those one sees winding through the alleys of little villages between mills and troughs—herds of small cattle either sold or led to pasture, comings and goings of charcoal burners and lumberjacks, peddlers who ventured all the way from the edge of the Borderlands. Then, as one went deeper into the haphazard solitudes, even those little human creakings in the hollow paths died away, and after the day's vast white emptiness, at dusk, free-roaming animals would take final possession of the land, for this clearing in the woods was accommodating and familiar to them, especially to those traveling far and wide; one would often hear, behind a nearby bend, a herd galloping over the rocks, or see, in the distance, a boar and sow grunting with pleasure as they ambled along the path, followed by a whole procession of their young; and on moving into the subtler light, one's heart would beat slightly faster: the Road—wild and prickly with grass, its pavement overtaken by nettles, blackthorn, and sloes—suddenly seemed to confuse eras rather than cross lands, as if it might emerge, in the semi-darkness of the thicket smelling of dewy thistle

trot de route, un sanglier avec sa laie et toute la file des mar-
cassins : et alors on avançait le cœur battant un peu dans la
lumière plus fine : on eût dit que soudain la Route ensau-
vagée, crépue d'herbe, avec ses pavés sombrés dans les orties,
les épines noires, les prunelliers, mêlait les temps plutôt qu'elle
ne traversait les pays, et que peut être elle allait déboucher,
dans le clair-obscur de hallier qui sentait le poil mouillé et
l'herbe fraîche, sur une de ces clairières où les bêtes parlaient
aux hommes.

À se défendre ainsi tout seul — au travers de ces longues
périodes où les hommes avaient cessé de rouler sur son lit
caillouteux — contre l'assaut des arbres, des bêtes, des plantes
sauvages, le Perré avait dû beaucoup composer : la belle ordon-
nance sévère de la route qui avait traversé ces pays en étrangère
s'était défaite. Comme les conquérants qui se sont tant bien
que mal adaptés en prenant les mœurs et le vêtement du pays
conquis, en passant des friches aux pays de forêts, aux marais,
aux collines caillouteuses, elle s'était incorporé quelque chose
de la substance même du pays traversé, au point d'en deve-
nir presque méconnaissable, et si parfois nous la maudissions
dans ses méchantes humeurs, il y avait pourtant un charme
à la trouver ainsi variée et changeante, toute imprégnée des
longues intimités de la solitude, laissant couler en nous à me-
sure les songes vagues et envahissants du grand chemin, les
odeurs de plantes et les bruits de bêtes, laissant les branches
mouillées nous fouetter le visage quand nous traversions les
bois, ou toute la poussière des plaines de sable nous blanchir.
Dans les campagnes crayeuses, son pavage clair, sous le trem-
blé léger des ombelles sèches qui se balançaient au long des
joints du dallage, conservait une netteté de ruban bien coupé,
courant droit à travers l'étendue ; devant soi, à la crête des
mouvements de terrain, on voyait onduler jusque très loin le
coup d'ongle de sa trace claire. Ces jours-là, sa netteté sèche et
éventée, sa voie confortable et droite, en nous promettant une

and fresh grass, onto one of those clearings where animals spoke to men.

To hold its own all by itself—throughout those long periods in which men had stopped crossing its stony bed—against the assault of trees, animals, and wild plants, the Embankment must have compromised a good amount: the strictly ordered layout of the road, which had traversed those lands like a foreigner, had come undone. Like those conquerors who have somehow adjusted to their surroundings by adopting the customs and dress of the conquered land, by going from fallow fields to forests, swamps, and rocky hills, the road had integrated something of the very substance of the traversed land, so much so that it had become nearly unrecognizable, and if we sometimes disparaged it for its bad humors, there was still charm in finding it so varied and mutable, steeped in such deep intimacy with solitude, in letting faint and invasive dreams of the open road flow into us along with the smells of plants and noises of animals, and in letting the damp branches of the woods whip our faces or all the dust of the sandy plains whiten our skin. In the chalky countryside, the pale pavement, under the slight tremble of dry umbels drifting along the grooves of the slabs, retained the sharpness of a finely trimmed ribbon, stretching straight across the expanse; from hilltops, the pavement's clear nail-like trace could be seen rippling into the distance. In those days, its blunt and coarse sharpness, its smooth and straight way, promising us an easy walk, added something to the weather's lovely blue. By the gorges, the path was often merely a dried-up riverbed, cut by fallen rocks, crumbled into pieces by mudslides, sometimes cracked open, exposing the loose sharp-edged stones of its base layers—a woeful rocky track that made horses balk. But I found this secluded path especially charming when, sometimes for entire days, it entered the forests. The pavement had long ago disappeared under a humus of yellow leaves,

étape facile, ajoutait quelque chose au bleu du beau temps. Au flanc des gorges, coupée d'éboulis, disloquée par les glissements de terrain, ouverte en deux parfois jusqu'à la pierraille coupante de ses fondations, ce n'était souvent qu'un lit de torrent à sec, une mauvaise coulée caillouteuse où les chevaux bronchaient. Mais surtout me plaisait ce chemin perdu quand, des jours entiers parfois, il s'engageait dans les forêts. Le pavé depuis longtemps avait disparu ici sous un humus de feuilles jaunies, un terreau noir et fin où le pied s'enfonçait sans aucun bruit. Le pas des chevaux sous les voûtes vertes s'étouffait aussi soudainement qu'on passait du soleil à l'ombre ; nous nous glissions en file indienne dans le brusque silence, sous la pluie fraîche et lente des sous-bois mouillés. Cette voie forestière perdue, sous son gazon fin parfois rougi de fraises, avec ses passées de bêtes, ses flaques d'eau noire, son odeur de mousse humide et de champignon frais, paraissait si abandonnée, si entièrement reprise par la sauvagerie des bois qu'on luttait difficilement contre l'impression qu'elle allait d'un instant à l'autre finir là en impasse, que les arbres allaient se refermer sur sa fente étroite, mais la digue de pierre, le mur invisible que le chemin enfonçait sous lui dans le sol, avait contenu obstinément l'assaut de la forêt, et la Route indéfiniment s'enfonçait, amicale et vaguement fée, filtrant à travers le sous-bois sa lumière calme et rassurant d'éclaircie, pas à pas écartant devant nous comme une main le rideau des branches.

Des pays qu'elle traversait, il me reste une image flottante, pareille à celle que pourrait laisser, plutôt qu'une terre ferme, avec tout ce que le mot implique de précis, de mesurable et de délimité, le souvenir par exemple d'un ciel de nuages, avec ses masses confuses et brouillées, sa dérive lente au fil des heures, la montée de signes de ses ombres d'orage, et cette manière rapide qu'il a de virer tout entier du clair au sombre. Quand il se découvrait au loin, du haut d'une colline, il se disposait par grandes taches aux bords effrangés qui s'amincissaient et se

in fine black fertile ground where feet sank without a sound. Under the green canopy, the horses' gaits were hushed as suddenly as a sunny spot might turn into shade; we'd slip into the abrupt silence one by one, in the fresh and slow rain of the dewy undergrowth. This secluded forest path, beneath its sharp grass sometimes stained red with strawberries, with its animal tracks, its puddles of black water, and its smell of damp moss and fresh mushrooms, appeared so forgotten, so entirely overtaken by the wilderness of the woods that one strenuously had to fight the impression that it would, at any given moment, lead to a dead end, that the trees would close in on its narrow crack; but the stone dike, the invisible wall which the path buried beneath it, had firmly contained the forest's assault, and the Road, amiable and vaguely magical, faded endlessly into the distance, as the sunny spell of its calm and reassuring light filtered through the undergrowth, step by step parting the curtain of branches before us like a hand.

Of the land it traversed, a floating image remains with me, similar to what might be left not by a piece of solid earth, with all that the phrase implies of specificity, measurability, and demarcation, but by the memory of, for instance, a sky of clouds with its faint and blurred masses, its slow drift through the hours, the rising signs of its stormy shadows, and that swift way it has of veering from fair to overcast. When it appeared in the distance, from the top of a hill, it was arranged in large patches with frayed edges that tapered off and melted into the edge of the horizon in confused strata, eventually blending into a darker circle that cast a shadow over the view: patches gloomier in the forests, clearer in the fields of grass, smoky gray and trembling in the steamy swamps: it all evoked a haunting impression of heavy stagnation. Yet it wasn't so much wilderness that it brought to mind as a return to wilderness; sometimes it looked like a shore whose tide came in to coat and wash over the leveling work that

fondaient au bord de l'horizon en strates confuses, finalement mêlées dans un cerne plus foncé qui fermait le regard : taches plus sombres des forêts, plus claires des plaines d'herbes, gris fumé et tremblé de vapeur des marais : l'ensemble évoquait une impression obsédante de stagnation lourde. Pourtant ce n'était pas tant à la sauvagerie qu'il faisait penser que plutôt à un retour vers la sauvagerie ; on aurait dit parfois une grève où la marée est venue recouvrir et délaver des travaux de terrassement déjà commencés. Les traces de vie n'en étaient pas absentes, et particulièrement le long de la Route que nous suivions ; mais la prise de l'homme sur ce glacis entre les terres pacifiées du Royaume et les contrées barbares s'était visiblement desserrée, à mesure que les vagues d'invasion devenaient plus fréquentes. Les signes de l'incendie, du pillage et de la mort violente n'y manquaient pas : çà et là des abatis tout récents coupaient la route, pointait la termitière noire d'une meule brûlée, ou bien, au milieu du rectangle vide d'un défrichement déjà repris par les chardons et les orties, on voyait se dresser la carcasse d'une ferme incendiée. Mais ces rencontres gardaient plutôt le caractère d'accidents isolés, auxquels l'œil ne se résignait pas d'avance, comme lorsqu'on s'est mis en tête, une fois pour toutes, qu'on traverse un pays « dévasté par la guerre » ; ces décombres charbonneux s'isolaient toujours vivement et sinistrement du paysage intact, comme un troupeau ou une grange calcinées par la foudre au milieu de la verdure de juin : plutôt qu'une campagne saccagée par l'invasion, on aurait cru parfois traverser une contrée aux étés anormalement orageux. Non, ce qui engourdissait ces campagnes peuplées de mauvais rêves, ce n'était pas la griffe appesantie d'un fléau, c'était plutôt un retrait souffreteux, une espèce de veuvage triste ; l'homme avait commencé à assujettir ces étendues vagues, puis il s'était lassé d'y mordre, et maintenant même le goût de maintenir sa prise avait pourri ; il s'était fait partout un reflux, un repli chagrin.

had already begun. The traces of life weren't gone—especially along the Road we followed—but man's hold on that glacis between the Kingdom's peaceful lands and the savage regions had visibly loosened, even as the waves of invasion grew more frequent. Signs of fire, pillage, and violent death remained: here and there ramparts of newly felled trees cut through the road, exposed the black termite mound of a burnt millstone, or perhaps in the middle of an empty rectangular clearing overtaken by thistles and nettles, the towering carcass of a burned-down farm would come into view. But those junctions kept the character of isolated events, to which the eye did not resign itself before—as when one has determined, once and for all, that one is crossing a land "devastated by the war"; that sooty rubble tended to isolate itself quickly and mournfully from the unscathed landscape, like a herd or barn scorched by lightning in the midst of June's greenery: rather than a land sacked by invasion, it sometimes seemed like a region affected by unusually stormy summers. No, what numbed those lands populated by unpleasant dreams wasn't the burdensome mark of a plague but a sickly retreat, a kind of depressing widowhood; man had begun to subjugate those vague expanses, then grew bored of sinking his teeth into the land, and now even his taste for keeping a hold on it had soured; everything had ebbed away in melancholy withdrawal. The clearcuttings in the forests, which one glimpsed from time to time, had lost their sharp angles, their clean edges: now bristly bushes overtook the clearings in broad daylight, concealing the naked trunks up to their first branches. The cultivated patches disappeared, like a pond drained to the bottom, leaving behind old sunken fences in the tall grass and a ring undulating with wild plants, pricked by white mullein and poppies. Of the small clusters of low-thatched cottages that had spread into the wilderness, flanked by their barns and haylofts, only the roofs could be seen or rather only their discolored beams bearded

Les coupes dans les forêts, qu'on apercevait de loin en loin, avaient perdu leurs angles vifs, leurs entailles nettes : maintenant une broussaille hirsute y menait son sabbat dans le plein jour des clairières, cachant les troncs nus jusqu'aux premières branches. Les taches cultivées se résorbaient, à la manière d'un étang qu'on vide par le fond, abandonnant autour d'elles les anciennes clôtures sombrées dans l'herbe haute, et tout un cerne ondulant de plantes sauvages, piqué de bouillons blancs et de coquelicots. Des petits groupes de chaumières basses qui avaient essaimé de loin en loin dans les friches, flanquées de leurs étables et de leurs greniers à foin, on n'apercevait plus que les toits ou plutôt leurs solives délavées encore barbues de chaume pourri ; déjà les battait jusqu'aux chéneaux la marée des plantes laineuses et ternes des décombres. Rien ne serrait le cœur, dans les clos autrefois labourés, où les îlots de pommiers reposaient maintenant le bord même de leur couronne sur le bouillonnement des herbes folles, comme l'émeute servile de ces plantes lépreuses, poilues et griffues, couleur de poussière, qui vivent des déchets de l'homme et qu'il tient très au large de ses hautes enceintes sarclées. Elles menaient leur ronde maintenant, pleines d'escargots et de couleuvres, autour du puits, du four et du lavoir, soufflant aux murs lézardés une fraîcheur malsaine de cave. Quelquefois, quand nous passions en vue d'une de ces épaves déjà sombrées dans les remous de l'écume verte, une curiosité triste nous écartait un moment de la Route, et, par les fenêtres arrachées, nous jetions un coup d'œil dans les pièces vides. Un grand jour blanc, sinistre, y tombait des toits crevés, faisant cligner comme un oiseau de nuit la caverne violée de la profonde maison paysanne, avec ses secrets pauvres et compliqués, le rencoignement peureux de son alcôve, ses caches à provisions, avec le suint de ses murs fumeux, épaissement frottés de peau humaine, la longue coulée de suie froide de sa cheminée, et, dans l'appentis carrelé de rouge, les pots à lait ébréchés encore pendus à leurs pitons

with rotten straw; the tide of the rubble's wooly, dull plants was already beating against their eaves. Nothing wrung the heart more, in the enclosed plots of once plowed land, where the islets of apple trees now lowered the very edge of their crowns onto the wild bubbling grass, than the servile revolt of those leprous plants, fuzzy and prickly, the color of dust, that live off man's waste and which he keeps far from his high pristine walls. Full of snails and garter snakes, the plants now led around the well, oven, and washhouse, exhaling a moldy coolness like a cellar's onto the cracked walls. Sometimes, when we came within sight of one of those wrecks already submerged in foamy green eddies, a sad curiosity momentarily took us away from the Road, and through the smashed windows, we'd glance into the empty rooms. A sinister white light would fall through the ruptured roofs and make the desecrated cave of the sunken farmhouse blink like a night bird, with its pitiful and intricate secrets, the fearful corner in its alcove, its store of supplies, with the grease of its smoky walls thickly rubbed with human skin, the long stream of cold soot from its chimney, and, in the red tiled outhouse, the chipped milk cans still hanging by their handles above the rusted churn. We no longer felt the sense of irreversible aging that cast a shadow over us when we crossed the countryside of the Kingdom: rather—in that land of mute and muffled roofs, where not a dog barked, not a cart jolted in the morning—we were overcome by a physical discomfort at once violent and subdued, the feeling of being led astray in a dreamland that wakes inexplicably late.

Despite the shelter they could provide us on occasion, we never liked camping near those areas touched by taboo. I remember one night we made a stop in one of those evacuated hamlets near the edge of a wood. Three or four giant elms crushed the little triangular space with their shadows: between the trunks, a few slate benches warded off the tall grass like

au-dessus de la baratte pourrie. Ce n'était plus comme quand on traversait les campagnes du Royaume, le sentiment du vieillissement sans remède qui nous assombrissait là : c'était, dans ces campagnes aux toits sourds et muets, sans un aboiement de chien, sans un cahotement matinal de charrette, un malaise physique à la fois diffus et violent, le sentiment d'être fourvoyé en rêve dans un pays qui se lève inexplicablement tard.

Malgré l'abri qu'ils pouvaient encore parfois offrir, nous n'aimions jamais camper près de ces lieux touchés d'interdit. Je me souviens qu'un soir nous fîmes halte dans un de ces hameaux évacués qui s'adossait à une lisière de bois. Trois ou quatre ormes géants écrasaient de leur ombre la petite place triangulaire : entre les troncs quelques bancs d'ardoise écartaient encore les hautes herbes comme des pierres tombales — dans un coin, un rouleau était resté basculé à l'ombre, enfoui jusqu'à ses brancards levés (on voyait partout ces lourds rouleaux de pierre, qu'on s'était découragé d'emmener, écarter les jambes très haut au-dessus de l'herbe dans les cours de ferme, une meule au cou). Les chevaux entravés, nous fîmes quelques pas indécis dans le foin suri qui nous montait jusqu'au ventre, ne nous décidant pas à allumer le feu, mal à l'aise sous le regard des fenêtres veuves qui nous suivaient sous le couvert de leurs orbites charbonneuses, puis, sans même nous consulter, nous nous remîmes en selle, et nous nous enfonçâmes dans la forêt.

Pourtant, si apparents que fussent les signes de l'abandon, l'homme n'avait pas complètement évacué ces solitudes. Seulement, comme il arrive lorsque la sécurité s'en va, il s'était fait un changement dans ses gîtes et ses allures qui donnait aux rencontres un caractère louche, passablement inquiétant. Les signes d'activité ancienne qui jalonnaient encore la route — parcelles encloses, bergeries, moulins, villages abandonnés — , toutes ces éraflures encore luisantes de la trace humaine où nous nous repérions, tout cela semblait à la race singulière dont nous recoupions ici et là les passées devenu

tombstones—in one corner, a roller had remained toppled over in the shade, buried up to its raised tow bar (we saw those heavy stone rollers everywhere, which were too big to take and whose legs stretched well above the grass in the farmyards, a millstone round the neck). The horses tethered, we took a few tentative steps into the spoiled hay, which rose up to our stomachs, before deciding not to light a fire, ill at ease under the widowed windows whose gaze followed us through their sooty eye sockets, then, without a word, we got back on our saddles and disappeared into the forest.

Yet, however apparent the signs of abandon, man hadn't entirely evacuated those solitudes. Only, as happens when a sense of safety slips away, a change had come to pass in his dwellings and appearance, which lent the junctions a seedy, rather troubling character. The signs of past activity that still punctuated the road—enclosed plots, sheepfolds, mills, deserted villages—all those abrasions that still gleamed with human traces and guided our way, all of that seemed, to the singular people whose path we crossed here and there, as suspicious as an unknown creature's tracks or feces to a forest animal. When rising smoke came into view, it was always well beyond the Road, sometimes leagues away, over the summits of bald rocks, or over hills that raised their shoulders behind forests, where one can often see the blaze of hunters' campfires or charcoal burners' wood piles: that enigmatic smoke in the evening, ascending above those high lands, hardly suggested a warm bed and steaming soup, and before deciding where to set up camp we'd assess how far away and in what direction the smoke rose. Even during the day, we couldn't escape the impression that we were moving between two invisible defense lines. The silhouettes we sometimes saw looming in the distance or stealing into the thickets didn't evoke travelers along their way: their mysterious and closed-off manner, and their aversion to being approached, was reminiscent of a tribe

aussi suspect qu'à une bête des bois les brisées ou les fientes d'une bête d'une autre espèce. Quand on voyait s'élever des fumées, c'était toujours très au large de la Route, parfois à des lieues, sur des sommets de roches chauves, ou sur les collines qui levaient l'épaule derrière les forêts, là où on voit brûler d'habitude les feux de camp des chasseurs ou les meules des charbonniers : ces fumées énigmatiques qui montaient dans le soir sur les lieux hauts ne parlaient guère de lit préparé et de soupe fumante, et nous interrogions longuement des yeux, avant de choisir l'emplacement de la couchée, leur distance et leur direction. Même de jour, l'impression ne s'effaçait jamais qu'on défilait entre deux lignes de guet invisibles. Les silhouettes qu'on voyait parfois se profiler au loin sur la route ou se faufiler dans les taillis n'évoquaient pas des voyageurs en chemin : leur allure indécise et peu franche, et le peu de souci qu'elles montraient d'être abordées, faisaient penser plutôt à une tribu en maraude aux confins de son territoire, ou aux gens qui battent l'estrade le long des grèves de mer. Hal, qui se sentait en sympathie avec ces flâneurs distants de la forêt, avait le don de les mettre assez souvent en confiance : quelquefois, ils s'enhardissaient jusqu'à s'asseoir un moment auprès de notre feu de camp, et nous déchiffrions par bribes la vie clairsemée qui couvait autour de nous. Il s'était formé là à l'écart un dépôt humain très mélangé — nomades coupés de leur gros qui s'étaient terrés dans des clairières en groupes consanguins de quelques familles (bien qu'ils eussent pris la langue du Royaume et des bribes de ses coutumes, on les reconnaissait à leurs huttes de bois qu'ils bâtissaient rondes, avec un toit conique de bardeaux, et qui n'étaient que des tentes de rondins) miliciens des Marches que l'ordre d'évacuation n'avait pas touchés dans leurs fortins perdus et qui régentaient comme des fiefs les petites communautés de trappeurs, de sabotiers et de voleurs de chevaux venues chercher asile derrière leurs palissades de bois — cadets aussi des fermes libres des

marauding at the borders of its territory, or people getting the lay of the land along the sea. Hal, who sympathized with those far-off wanderers of the forest, had the gift of gaining their trust rather often: sometimes they worked up the courage to join us at our campfire, and in bits we'd decipher the sparse life that brooded around us. A mixed assortment of people had formed there—nomads cut off from their community who, split into bands of intermarried families, had sought refuge in the glades (though they'd adopted the language of the Kingdom and bits of their customs, they were recognizable by their round wooden huts, which were mere tents of logs, with shingled conic roofs), militiamen from the Borderlands who, in their remote forts, hadn't received the evacuation order, and, like fiefs, controlled the small communities of trappers, clog makers, and horse thieves seeking asylum behind their palisades of wood—youths, too, from the abandoned farms of cleared-out land who had developed a taste for adventure, and, rather than follow their elder brothers to the old Country that maintained its land registry so well, had picked up their guns and advanced into the forest. When we took up conversation with those little clans, half-hunter, half-pillager, who popped up here and there like wild plants, we were surprised to sense in their remarks how little they regretted leaving their old, comfortable lives to roam far away, slightly stunned by their freedom, on smooth new ground. Here the earth had turned green again and shaken itself awake, with a fresh coat, rid of the scrapes from its old, loosened straps, and man too was rejuvenated, set free in the haze of grass like a stallion, bucked up from trotting across the unwrinkled earth as if across a still-damp seashore.

As for the detachments that passed along the Road, their demeanor was neither hostile nor hateful; they were like pillagers of shipwrecks in view of what marched toward their downfalls: neutral—an armed and equipped troop, sure of

défrichements qui avaient pris là le goût de large, et, plutôt que de suivre leur aîné au vieux Pays qui tenait si bien son cadastre, avaient décroché leur fusil et gagné la forêt. Quand on prenait langue avec ces petits clans qui repoussaient çà et là comme des plantes folles, à demi-chasseurs, à demi-pillards, on était surpris de sentir à travers leurs propos avec combien peu de regrets ils avaient pris congé de la vie ancienne et confortable, et s'ébattaient maintenant au large, un peu étourdis de leur liberté, sur un sol lissé de neuf. Ici la terre avait reverdi, elle s'ébrouait, le poil frais, toute nette des écorchures de ses vielles sangles desserrées, et l'homme aussi rajeunissait, lâché dans la brume d'herbes comme un cheval entier, ragaillardi de marcher sur la terre sans rides comme sur une grève à peine ressuyée de la mer.

Vis-à-vis des détachements qui passaient de loin en loin au fil de la Route, leur attitude n'était pas hostile ni haineuse, elle était celle des pilleurs d'épaves vis-à-vis de ce qui défile en vue de leurs écueils : impartiale — une troupe bien armée et pourvue, sûre de sa route, pouvait croire traverser seulement une solitude giboyeuse — égarée, à court de vivres, ou désemparée par un accident, elle risquait le pire, car l'odeur du sang ici, comme dans la mer, voyageait loin ; la poudre et le plomb, les vêtements et les chevaux étaient des objets de furieuse convoitise, et, tant valait ce qu'il transportait, tant à peu près valait la vie du voyageur. L'embarras du cadavre vient d'habitude de tout ce qu'il traîne après lui de redoutablement enchevêtré : il ressemble à ces flotteurs de liège auxquels sont accrochés des filets de pêche : y toucher, c'est tirer au jour maille après maille un grouillement à chavirer la barque. Ici, où les amarres étaient coupées, les bouchons dansaient, et la mort avait cessé de poser des questions : on rencontrait de temps en temps au bord du chemin de petits tas de pierres allongés auxquels la coutume de la Route était d'ajouter seulement au passage un caillou, geste d'absolution distraite qui tenait quittes à la

its way, might think it's crossing a mere solitude abounding in game—lost, running low on supplies, or discouraged by a setback, the soldiers risked everything, for here the smell of blood, as in the sea, traveled long distances; powder and shot, clothes and horses were furiously sought after, and a traveler's life was worth more or less what he carried. The shame of a corpse usually comes from the dreadful entanglements it drags behind it: bodies are like those corks attached to fishing nets: merely touching the mesh would create such a jumble as to capsize the boat. Here where the mooring lines were cut, the corks danced, and death stopped asking questions: now and then we encountered little piles of rocks spread along the path's edge; the custom of the Road was to add a stone in passing, a gesture of distracted absolution that cleared the dead man of his memory and the murderer of his motives: this little moraine of men that grew little by little along the path didn't weigh on memory like cemetery grounds, and didn't give way to reflection. It made the wind and open waters murmur along the Road, like boats moored to a dock, and when it spread beneath the trees, one could sit there undisturbed to collect one's thoughts or get one's bearings: there was a sense of repose in those faint graves, which put life so at ease and had so little to see to that they were matters of neither testimony nor duty.

* * *

Along the Embankment, we sometimes encountered women. They traveled in twos or threes—almost never alone, almost always on horseback—though once we passed two on foot: two dark, fragile shadows, far ahead on the path, whose heavy boots made them limp like lame birds: they held hands in silence and—I remember it was around Easter—nibbled on

fois le mort de sa mémoire et le meurtrier de ses raisons :
cette petite moraine d'hommes qui se déposait peu à peu
au long de la voie ne pesait pas au souvenir comme la terre
des cimetières et ne donnait pas à penser. Elle faisait au long
de la Route un murmure de vent et d'eaux libres, comme les
barques amarrées au bord d'un quai, et lorsqu'elle s'allongeait
sous les arbres, on s'y asseyait sans gêne pour se reconnaître
ou s'orienter : il y avait un repos dans ces tombes légères qui
mettaient la vie si à l'aise, et ne se chargeaient si peu que ce
fût ni de témoignage, ni de commission.

* * *

Au long du Perré, nous rencontrions parfois des femmes. Elles
allaient par deux, par trois — presque jamais seules — à che-
val presque toujours — pourtant une fois nous en dépassâmes
deux qui allaient à pied : deux silhouettes noires et fragiles,
loin devant nous sur le chemin, auxquelles les pesantes bottes
de voyage donnaient un sautillement d'oiselet boiteux : elles
se tenaient par le doigt sans rien dire et — je me souviens que
c'était le temps de Pâques — elles mordillaient une branche
fleurie : les bois dans le brouillard de verdure jaune étaient
pleins d'appels de coucous, mais c'étaient ces bouches seules
tout à coup sur le chemin plein de fondrières et d'eaux neuves
qui nous apprenaient que la terre fleurissait. La Route, où elles
vivaient dans le remous du long voyage, leur avait donné peu
à peu une espèce d'uniforme ; presque toutes portaient les
épaisses bottes plissées sur la cheville, les braies lacées, le petit
poignard et le corselet de cuir qui les enserrait rudement de la
taille aux poignets ; mais elles allaient tête nue et les cheveux
libres, une lourde crinière chaude qui leur tombait jusqu'aux
reins, pleine d'épines et d'odeurs sauvages. Il n'y avait rien de
vil ni de vulgaire dans ces rencontres. Elles étaient venues

blossoms: the woods in the fog of yellow foliage were full of cuckoo calls, but it was those mouths, suddenly heard on the path full of potholes and freshly fallen rain, that told us the earth was in bloom. The Road, where they lived in the whirlwind of a long journey, had little by little given them a sort of uniformity; nearly all of them wore cinched braies, thick boots scrunched at the ankles, a small dagger, and leather bodices that harshly tightened around the waist up to the wrists; they never covered their heads and always wore their hair down, warm, heavy manes that fell to their lower backs, full of thorns and wild smells. There was nothing vile or vulgar about these encounters. They sometimes came from afar, upon learning which travelers were passing through, not to live off them—they asked for nothing and almost never accepted gifts, and when they did, it was on a strange whim or according to a secret set of rules, which revealed their dignified ways—but to live with them, or rather near and like them, on the Road, a kind of awakened path where one could breathe like nowhere else: they were like those sea birds that momentarily sway under the wind of a ship before abandoning one for another, as if it were the journey's fresh, foamy eddy that enchanted them rather than the traveler himself. Almost all of them were beautiful, in a vigorous and slightly heavy way; they resembled those brazen-eyed farm girls one might see riding back from the water trough at nightfall—but the Road had matured them, or perhaps its call, deep in the earthy country, had reached only those who could run there with lighter blood. Their contempt for the serfs of the land, who embraced working animals in their smoky beds at night, was profound: it was an almost spiritual contempt for the wallowing dwellers of the feudal land, which they harbored with something of the haughtiness of a noble's servant who has chosen to breathe the emanations of an elected race. They spoke little and feared nothing, came with sage and subtle

parfois de très loin, ayant entendu dire quels voyageurs passaient sur le chemin, non pour vivre d'eux — car elles ne demandaient rien et le don même n'était jamais accepté qu'avec de bizarres caprices, ou bien selon des règles cachées, qui laissaient entrevoir une intégrité farouche — , mais pour vivre avec eux, ou plutôt à portée d'eux et à leur guise, dans cette espèce de sillage éveillé qu'était la Route et où on respirait comme nulle part : on pensait quelquefois à ces oiseaux de mer qui se balancent un moment sous le vent des navires, mais les abandonnent l'un pour l'autre, comme si le frais remous d'écume du voyage les captivait plutôt que le voyageur. Presque toutes étaient belles, d'une beauté drue et un peu lourde ; elles ressemblaient à ces filles de paysans, aux yeux hardis dans la nuit tombante, qu'on voit monter à cru les chevaux revenant de l'abreuvoir — mais la Route les avait affinées, ou peut-être son appel avait-il touché dans le fond de ces campagnes terreuses seulement ce qui pouvait y courir encore de sang plus léger. Leur mépris pour la race serve de la terre, qui étreignait chaque soir dans son lit enfumé des bêtes de labour, était insondable : c'était le mépris d'un ordre presque spirituel pour le tout-venant vautré de la glèbe, et un peu la morgue du serviteur de noble qui a choisi de respirer tout le jour l'émanation d'une race élue. Elles parlaient peu — ne craignaient pas — étaient de sage et subtil conseil pour les dangers de la route — et on pouvait si on voulait traiter en camarades, comme des hôtes de voyage d'un jour, ces alertes et taciturnes petits compagnons bottés de cuir qui savaient passer le mors à une bête et jurer entre leurs dents comme un homme — mais quelquefois, à l'étape, quand la nuit s'était épaissie autour du lit de braises rouges — la seule coquetterie qu'elles avaient c'était de toujours *choisir* — une bouche cherchait votre bouche dans le noir avec une confiance têtue de bête douce qui essaie de lire sur le visage de son maître, et c'était soudain toute une femme, chaude, dénouée comme une

advice about the road's dangers—and, if one wished, one could treat them like comrades, like companions for the day, those vigilant, reserved travelers with leather boots, who could bridle a horse and swear through their teeth like a man—but now and then, when the night thickened over the bed of red embers, a mouth would search for yours in the dark—their sole coquetry was always their insistence on *choosing*—with the stubborn determination of an animal trying to read its master's face, and suddenly an entire woman would appear, warm, loose as rain, heavy as formless night, who'd let herself sink into your arms. When we set off on the road, chastity did not rule over us, and we'd receive those rough godsends as they came. Since then—something about those encounters felt incomplete, clumsy, and tender at once, and they have endured in my memory without a trace of impurity—I've sometimes thought those wanderers, with their sweet, billowing hair, may have been ridding themselves—and yet this is strange to say—*faute de mieux*—of the encumberment of the female body, presenting it in the dark with a sort of humble submission, intent on communicating only through the warm thickness of their flesh. What they sought, what they clumsily strove to attain, what kept them so patiently awake at night was not the travelers on the Road, but perhaps a reflection of more distant things—of where the Road would lead them— which they passionately projected onto them. Woman is more eager than man to be swept away by certain gusts that rise on earth, but her body's warm darkness weighs her down, and it sometimes comes to pass that, out of impatience with her body that deprives her of complete lucidity, she surrenders it as one might take a shortcut. No one ever seemed entirely unaware of this, and even the coarsest men reemerged from those chance embraces touched fleetingly by a sort of rough delicacy: on saying goodbye in the morning, they treated them not as women but as companions, as loyal comrades.

pluie, lourde comme une nuit défaite, qui se laissait couler entre vos bras. Quand nous allions, la chasteté ne nous était pas une règle et nous prenions comme elles nous venaient ces aubaines brusques du chemin. Quelquefois, depuis — car il y avait dans ces rencontres quelque chose à la fois d'inachevé, de gauche et de tendre, et de tenace au souvenir qui n'en gardait jamais rien d'impur — j'ai pensé que ces errantes aux doux cheveux soudain répandus se donnaient peut-être — et pourtant c'est étrange à dire — *faute de mieux* — embarrassées de ce corps de femme qu'elles offraient dans le noir avec une espèce de soumission humble, vouées à ne connaître jamais qu'à travers sa chaude épaisseur. Ce qu'elles cherchaient, ce qu'elles voulaient gauchement rejoindre, ce qui les tenait éveillées les nuits dans une si longue patience, ce n'était pas ceux qui passaient sur la Route, c'était peut-être un reflet sur eux passionnément recueilli de choses plus lointaines — de cela seulement peut-être où la Route les conduisait. La femme tressaille plus vite que l'homme à ce qu'il passe d'emportant dans certains souffles qui se lèvent sur la terre, mais la ténèbre chaude de son corps lui pèse, et il arrive que par impatience de ce qu'il empêche en elle de tout à fait lucide, elle le donne comme on coupe par le chemin le plus court. Il me semble que personne ne s'y méprenait jamais tout à fait, et que même les plus grossiers se relevaient de ces étreintes de hasard touchés un instant d'une espèce de délicatesse rude : les traitant, à l'instant de l'adieu matinal, non en femmes mais en compagnons d'une étape et en loyaux camarades. Elles ne cherchaient jamais à retarder ou à retenir, et, au matin, elles servaient l'ami d'une nuit qui se harnachait avec une adresse de page et des gestes tout ennoblis de ne se permettre aucune familiarité trouble, sachant ce qui est du lit, et ce qui est pour l'homme d'un autre ordre — et suivre le mâle bravement dans sa répugnance à les mêler.

The women never sought to delay or keep them, and the next day, they'd help their one-time lovers pack up with the skill of a squire, adopting ennobled gestures to avoid any ambiguous familiarity, knowing the difference between what belongs in bed and what is, for man, of a different order—and bravely following his repugnance at mixing the two.

I think of them now and then—it's strange: how close they were to us, how brotherly—with a sort of solemn tenderness. No doubt they still wander parts of the Road where no one goes anymore, those restless bacchantes—half-courtesan, half-sibyl—whose desire sought to babble another language, forever unfit, as they've become, to compromise with a banal life, their big eyes, proud and sad, like a dried-up well on a deserted path—bearing the regret and widowhood of that small, fragile society of women that sometimes suspends itself momentarily, modeling itself on the male order in the places he lives and closes himself off in austerity; and which in its own way also flourishes, barren as it is, in its strange virtues, with a strong and persistent smell. Unable to touch and attain, they gave, humbly. They were lay sisters on a long journey, resigned to the more thankless tasks, yet incapable of sullying their hands and mouths with anything that didn't carnally align with a certain order they felt within their hearts. I remember their somber eyes and their faces raised strangely toward a kiss, as if it might illuminate them—and the gesture still comes back to me, as it came to us when we left them, with a sort of shy and pitiful tenderness, of kissing them on the forehead.

Je songe à elles quelquefois — c'est singulier : à certains instants si proches de nous si fraternelles — avec une espèce de grave tendresse. Sans doute errent-elles encore après de la Route coupée où il ne passe plus personne, ces bacchantes inapaisées dont le désir essayait de balbutier une autre langue — moitié courtisanes, moitié sibylles — inaptes pour jamais qu'elles sont devenues à composer avec la vie banale, leur grand œil fier et triste comme un puits tari sur le chemin désert — portant le regret et le veuvage de cette petite société de femmes — fragile — qui se suspend parfois un instant et se modèle à l'ordre mâle dans les lieux où il vit et se referme sur lui-même le plus austèrement ; et qui à sa manière aussi fleurit, toute stérile qu'elle est, en vertus étranges, au parfum tenace et fort. Faute de pouvoir toucher et tout à fait atteindre, elles donnaient, humblement. Elles étaient les converses du long voyage, résignées aux tâches plus pauvres, mais incapables de salir leurs mains et leur bouche à ce qui ne touchait pas charnellement à un certain ordre qu'elles pressentaient avec le cœur. Je me souviens de leurs yeux graves et de leur visage étrangement haussé vers le baiser comme vers quelque chose qui l'eût éclairé — et le geste me vient encore, comme il nous venait quand nous les quittions, avec une espèce de tendresse farouche et pitoyable, de les baiser sur le front.

Notes to the Text

The notes that follow draw extensively from Bernhild Boie's excellent Pléiade edition of Gracq's *Œuvres complètes*. Information about Gracq's original drafts comes from his archives at the Bibliothèque Nationale de France. All translations from the French in the notes and introduction are mine, unless otherwise noted.

Toward Urban Galvanization

erection—*priapée* in French. The word refers to a licentious or obscene poem or painting. Priapus was the god of fertility and was often depicted with an enormous phallus.

shaking off the unavoidable remoras—small fish also known as shark suckers or suckerfish. Merriam-Webster notes, "Ancient sailors believed remoras had the power to slow or even stop a ship by attaching themselves to it; the name *remora*, which means 'delay' in Latin, arose from this ancient superstition." The italicization of *"remoras"* is the first of many to come in the collection. In an interview with Jean-Louis Tissier, Gracq discussed the significance of his use of italics: "often they serve to emphasize a key word that's essential to the sentence ... to indicate that a word has a double meaning ... [or] to highlight an ironic meaning."

The Golden Age—a Surrealist film made by Luis Buñuel and Salvador Dalí. It was screened for the first time in 1930, at Montmartre's Studio 28, one of the first art house cinemas. Offended by the film's obscene and grotesque images, the far-right League of Patriots disrupted a later showing of the film by throwing ink on the screen, damaging furniture, and destroying Surrealist art on display in the lobby. The film was subsequently banned by the Board of Censors.

on the front steps of the Opera ... on a meadow-green ocean more convincing than nature—a series of images based on a collage published in the *Revue surréaliste* (no. 12, 1929, p. 46). The collage portrays a field, cows, and a pond in front of the Palais Garnier.

"This evening, to Circeto of the tall ice ..."—a reference to the penultimate paragraph of Rimbaud's prose poem "Devotion" in *Illuminations*. The full paragraph reads: "This evening to Circeto of the tall ice, greasy as fish, and lit up like the ten months of the red night,—(her heart of amber and spunk),—for my one prayer mute as those regions of night, that precedes exploits of gallantry more violent than this polar rubble" (trans. John Ashbery). In the context of the poem, it is possible to read Circeto as a reference to a woman, though Gracq takes it to be a city. The ambiguity of the name explains his hesitation to assert a definitive interpretation—"a phrase from a poem of Rimbaud's, which I may be misinterpreting." Indeed, Gracq adds a comma after "evening" to the original phrase.

Saint-Nazaire—a coastal city about 60 miles west of Gracq's hometown Saint-Florent-le-Vieil. Throughout his childhood, he and his family would stop by the city during vacations. Saint-Nazaire remained ever present in Gracq's memory. In *The Shape of a City*, he reflected: "For me, the true port ... has always been Saint-Nazaire ... it is an ocean door, where the wind from the expanse of water perpetually made ripples in the puddles on the Ville-ès-Martin boulevard."

Wells's giant Martians with their tripods—a reference to the aliens that invade earth in H.G. Wells's *The War of the Worlds*.

nave—*nef* in French, which can refer to a ship or the nave of a cathedral.

sailing iron cathedral—an image inspired by two of Gracq's memories of Saint-Nazaire. In 1926, when he was fifteen years old, he attended the launch of the *Île-de-France*, and from 1930 to 1932, he

witnessed the gradual construction of the liner *Normandie*, which measured 313 meters long and 39 meters tall.

poet's mastless scow—a reference to the final stanza of Baudelaire's verse poem "The Seven Old Men." The stanza goes as follows:

> Vainly my reason sought to take the helm—
> the gale made light of purpose and my soul
> went dancing on, an old and mastless scow
> dancing across a black and shoreless sea.
> *(trans. Richard Howard)*

de Chirico's hypnotized cities—a reflection of Gracq's lifelong fascination with de Chirico's paintings: "de Chirico captures in his paintings the *moment* between the second when the magic signal, the fatal, pronounced word, has just been given and the second when the walls of Jericho collapse ... with fifty years of hindsight, one comes to understand that the shadows projected by his arches and statues were never related to the sun, but rather to the light of an atomic mushroom cloud" (*Lettrines* [*Initial Capitals*]).

built by Amphion's harp—Amphion, along with his twin brother Zethus, fortified Thebes by building a wall. According to the myth, when Amphion played his lyre, the stone blocks magically moved into place.

destroyed by Jericho's trumpet—As recounted in Joshua, Jericho was the first city the Israelites attacked after entering Canaan. After seven days circling around the city, Joshua instructed his people to blow their trumpets until the walls came down. Gracq wrote "Toward Urban Galvanization" around the same time that the Royal Air Force launched its first attacks on the German base of submarines in the military port; the bombings would gradually devastate Saint-Nazaire.

The devil ... blowing up rooftops—a combination of the image of justice limping—from the French expression "la justice suit le crime d'un pied boiteux" ("justice follows crime with a lame foot")—and a literary reference to Alain-René Lesage's *The Devil Upon Two Sticks*. In the novel, set in Madrid, the demon Asmodeus removes the rooftops of bourgeois houses to reveal the secret lives of their inhabitants.

Venice

A city dear to Gracq and which he evokes in various other works, for instance in *Lettrines* (*Initial Capitals*): "the greatest charm of that ghost town is that it's still alive in a way that no other town is, all the faint sounds of its small, endearing life ... a footstep on the paving stones, a bucket that one fills, a drawn louver shutter, a conversation rising behind a wall, taking on a dramatic resonance and meaning in the deep silence."

Martinengo palace—one of three palaces named after the eponymous Venetian family.

Werther—an 1892 opera by Jules Massenet.

Philippine Trench—one of the deepest trenches in the ocean, located southeast of the Philippines.

Transbaikalia

Nonni, Kherlen, Selenga—rivers in Transbaikalia. Nonni crosses Manchuria, Selenga feeds into Lake Baikal, and Kherlen stretches across Mongolia and Manchuria.

The Cold Wind of the Night

This poem bears the same title as one of Leconte de Lisle's *Poèmes barbares* (*Barbaric Poems*).

Written in Water

The title of this poem refers to the inscription on John Keats's grave in Rome: "Here lies one whose name was writ in water."

Isabelle Elisabeth

In an interview with Jean Roudaut, Gracq explained the transition from "Isabelle" to "Elisabeth" and from "Beauty" to "Beast": "... in a short poem, like the one you're alluding to, sometimes a system of echoes that establishes itself between proper nouns guides the poem. In writing as I see it, sometimes sound, other times sense plays the role of the director."

Lermontov—Gracq translated Lermontov's "The Sail," originally published in Russian in 1831. One translation of that poem reads as follows:

> Amid the blue haze of the ocean
> A sail is passing, white and frail.
> What do you seek in a far country?
> What have you left at home, lone sail?
>
> The billows play, the breezes whistle,
> And rhythmically creaks the mast.
> Alas, you seek no happy future,
> Nor do you flee a happy past.
>
> Below the mirrored azure brightens,
> Above the golden rays increase—
> But you, wild rover, pray for tempests,
> As if in tempests there was peace!
> *(trans. Vladimir Nabokov)*

Vergiss Mein Nicht

Vergißmeinnicht is the German word for *myosotis*, commonly known as forget-me-nots. By splitting up the word, Gracq emphasizes the meaning of the title as the imperative "forget me not" (following an archaic German construction).

Unattainable

Gracq originally titled this poem "Les Aspects de la pyrogravure" ("Aspects of Pyrography").

Furnished Parlor

The setting of this poem resembles the strange interiors of Surrealist paintings and exhibitions. The collage effect of the poem recalls the technique Max Ernst employed in his paintings.

vespasiennes—public urinals also known as *pissoirs*. *Vespasiennes* could be found in the streets of Paris during the nineteenth century. The name comes from the Roman emperor Vespasian, who imposed a urine tax on public toilets.

curule chair—"a style of chair reserved in ancient Rome for the use of the highest government dignitaries and usually made like a camp-stool with curved legs," according to the *Encyclopedia Britannica*.

President Sadi-Carnot—Marie François Sadi Carnot (1837–94), elected president of France in 1887 and assassinated in 1894 by an Italian anarchist.

White Nights

The title of this poem is a reference to Dostoevsky's *White Nights*, published in 1848.

chanson de toile—a genre of lyric poetry popular in the twelfth and thirteenth centuries. The name—literally "web song"—suggests that the songs were originally sung by women weaving or embroidering.

Islands—islands of the Gulf of Finland, a popular summer destination for residents of Saint Petersburg (Petrograd at the time).

Robespierre

Saint-Just—president of the National Convention and a major advocate of the Reign of Terror. He was arrested and executed in the Thermidorian Reaction.

Jacques Roux—an unfrocked priest and one of the leaders of the *Enragés* (literally the "Enraged Ones"), which sought to establish a classless society. He stabbed himself after hearing that he would be tried for his extremist positions by the Revolutionary Tribunal.

the younger Robespierre—nickname of Augustin Bon Joseph de Robespierre, a member of the National Convention and Maximilien Robespierre's younger brother. When Maximilien was sentenced to death on 9 Thermidor (July 27, 1794), Augustin asked to share his brother's fate and was subsequently executed.

bundles of grain—Maximilien Robespierre carried a bouquet of wheat to the first national celebration of the Supreme Being on June 8, 1794. He intended for the Cult of the Supreme Being to replace Roman Catholicism as the state religion of the new French Republic.

The Trumpets of Aida

The title of this poem is a reference to the fanfare in the "Triumphal March" of Verdi's opera *Aida*.

Bulgar-Slayer emperor—the nickname of Basil II (958–1025), the emperor of Byzantium from 976 to 1025. He earned the name after leading extermination campaigns against the Bulgarian Empire.

Original Synthetic Unity of Apperception

This poem's title—akin to the surprising, misleading, and provocative titles of Surrealist paintings—refers to the sixteenth paragraph of the first book of Kant's *Critique of Pure Reason*.

Francis Jammes—a French poet (1868–1938) best known for his lyric poetry about the simple life in the countryside. Gracq later said of him: "No one has stammered as he has about the homely sweetness of old kitchens in the countryside, of the fresh and mopped red tiles, of the dog sleeping with his muzzle between his paws, of the after-dinner pipe lit on the front steps and under the wisteria, across from the well, in the summer twilight" (*Lettrines 2* [*Initial Capitals 2*]).

I have two large oxen in my stable—the first line of the popular song "Les Bœufs" ("The Oxen") by Pierre Dupont (1821–70).

Worldly Scandals

The original draft of this poem consisted of the second and third paragraphs, while the rest was added later. The penultimate paragraph was originally part of the poem "Justice."

Susquehanna River

Brest-Litovsk train station—the location where German and Soviet delegations (the latter led by Trotsky, Commissar of Foreign Affairs at the time) met in March of 1918 to negotiate a peace treaty.

Pleasant Morning Walk

The poem's title alludes to Rimbaud's verse poem "Bonne pensée du matin" ("Pleasant Morning Thought").

The Great Game

This poem, entitled "Par Exemple" ("For Example") in Gracq's original draft, alludes to a Surrealist-adjacent magazine of the same name published from 1928–29.

reverse side—*envers* in French. The two words *en vers* mean "in verse."

Ambiguous Departure

The draft of this poem bore the title "L'Embarcadère" ("The Pier" / "The Quay").

cast off—*lâchez-tout* (a noun), which refers to the release of mooring lines in the context of the poem. The word also recalls Breton's article "Lâchez tout" ("Leave Everything"), which ends with the following injunctions:

> Leave everything.
> Leave Dada.
> Leave your wife, leave your mistress.
> Leave your hopes and fears.
> Drop your kids in the middle of nowhere.
> Leave the substance for the shadow.
> Leave behind, if need be, your comfortable life and promising
>   future.
> Take to the highways.
> *(trans. Mark Polizzotti)*

Justice

Gracq's original title for the draft of this poem was "Croquis d'audience" ("Courtroom Sketch").

Truro

The title alludes to Cornwall's county town, which Gracq visited in 1933.

The Convent of the Pantocrator

This poem alludes to the monastery of the Pantocrator on Mount Athos in Greece, a site where women and female animals have been barred for over a thousand years.

On the Banks of Fine Bendemeer

The title is a reference to a line from Thomas Moore's poem "Lalla Rookh," published in 1817: "that bower on the banks of the calm Bendemeer."

Cortege

Men 40—horses 8—an indication of the carriage's capacity for purposes of mobilization, a practice applied to wooden freight trains up until the end of the Second World War.

The Good Inn

The title of this poem was originally "Parties at the House of Augustulus." The name "the Good Inn" appears in Breton's *Soluble Fish*: "I saw great lords with jabots of rain pass by on horseback one day, and I am the one who welcomed them at the Good Inn" (trans. Richard Seaver and Helen R. Lane).

Parties at the House of Augustulus

The poem was initially entitled "The Valley of Josaphat."

Romulus Augustulus, whose last name means the pejorative "little Augustus," was considered the last Western Roman emperor. He ruled for just a year, from 475 to 476.

balls of bluing—pods used for bleach before the invention of chemical detergents. Breton was struck by the pods' shape and bright color. In *Soluble Fish*, he wrote, "Elsewhere, in a farmyard probably, a woman is juggling with several balls of bluing, which burn in the air like fingernails" (trans. Seaver and Lane).

The Valley of Josaphat

This poem, written in Caen over the course of 1943 and based on Gracq's memory of his travels in Normandy, refers to the place of the Last Judgment according to Joel 4:2. Josaphat in Hebrew means "Yahweh has judged."

Paris at Dawn

Written in 1947, this poem evokes Paris in the immediate aftermath of the war.

Rastignac, from the top of Père-Lachaise—a reference to the end of Balzac's *Père Goriot*, in which Rastignac challenges Paris with the cry "À nous deux maintenant!" (literally, "to us two now!"). The scene takes place at dusk.

Parisian dream—a reference to Baudelaire's poem "Parisian Dream." The first part of the poem ends with the following stanza:

> And on these marvels as they moved
> there weighed (without a sound—
> the eye alone was master here)
> the silence of the Void.
> *(trans. Richard Howard)*

for Paris, as for the biblical sentinel, morning comes, and so does night—a reference to Isaiah 21:11–12: "'Sentinel, what of the night? Sentinel, what of the night?' The sentinel says: 'Morning comes, and also the night'" (New Revised Standard Version).

Moses

Gracq's drift along a slow and dark river becomes the subject of his short prose piece *The Narrow Waters*, which finds him in a boat drifting on the Èvre, a river that feeds into the Loire. The poem's title recalls

the biblical scene, as told in Exodus, of the infant Moses drifting in a basket along the Nile before being saved by the Pharaoh's daughter.

The Uplands of Sertalejo
While Sertalejo is a fictitious name, the landscapes evoked in this poem are based on the high plateaus of the Andes.

Jules Monnerot—a close friend of Gracq's. They attended the same high school, the Lycée Henri IV. A writer, journalist, and sociologist, Monnerot and George Bataille founded the Collège de Sociologie in 1938 and the literary review *Critique* in 1946.

The morning suspended ... from the blankets of fog—the description of this mountain finds an analogue in the volcano in Gracq's novel *The Opposing Shore*. In an interview with Jean-Louis Tissier, Gracq discusses his portrayals of mountains: "There are volcanos in my books, a large volcano in *The Opposing Shore*, and in *Abounding Freedom*, there are high plateaus with volcanos—the high plateaus of the Andes. What's striking about high mountains, and this was a shock to me, is the feeling that true mountains are those with permanent snow. Low mountains don't interest me much and the mountains of the lower Dauphiné not at all. One has the distinct feeling, in front of a mountain eternally covered with snow, that it's hanging from above rather than being rooted in the ground. That snowy zone seems suspended. I've never gone to see for myself because I don't climb much, but it maintains the dignity of something that has never been traversed."

Siesta in Dutch Flanders
Gracq particularly admired the landscapes of Dutch Flanders, which he visited during the war and shortly after. Suzanne Lilar (see note below) recalled his visit in "Julien Gracq en Flandre" ("Julien Gracq in Flanders"), in which she quotes a letter he sent her in the summer of 1950: "I was pleased to offer you this little text ... it concerns a land that is dear to you, I'm not sure I know it well, but it ended up

becoming a singular place for me where everything converges. There was a time when I dreamt of Lohengrin's swan and Elsa von Brabant—then, for no sane or strategic reason, the war led me to the banks of the Scheldt—and other meetings have brought me back over the past few months. In short, it's a very stimulating place for me. The three days I spent there in 1940 ... left a strange, lasting impression."

Madame S.L.—Suzanne Lilar, a Belgian writer who wrote in French. In 1949, she invited Gracq to Antwerp, where he gave his first lecture abroad—"Le Surréalisme et la Littérature contemporaine" ("Surrealism and Contemporary Literature"). Lilar became a lifelong friend.

Gomorrah

This poem recalls the first leg of a bike ride Gracq took from Caen to Clécy—both towns in Normandy—and finally to his hometown Saint-Florent-le-Vieil in May of 1944. Caen is the implied Gomorrah of the poem, as the city was destroyed by Allied bombing.

Forest of Cinglais—a forest to the east of the Orne and to the south of Caen. In May of 1944, an armed German division occupied the forest and the surrounding châteaux.

German hour—the *heure allemande* was Central European Time, two hours ahead of Paris time. The hour was enforced in all regions under the Third Reich's control.

Jaur—the only city in this poem that does not exist, though it corresponds to Clécy.

Aubrac

This poem's title brings us to a real place: the grassy basalt plateau south of Auvergne in the Massif Central. Gracq frequently returned to Aubrac in his later works, for instance in *Carnets du grand chemin* (*Notes from the Open Road*): "A subtle attraction, though hard to resist,

brings me back, year after year, time and time again, toward the high, naked surfaces both basalt and limestone—of the middle and southern parts of the Central Massif: Aubrac, the Cézallier, the *planèzes*, the Causses."

Viadène—a granite plateau south of Aubrac.

Causses—limestone plateaus in Mende, southeast of Aubrac.

References

Blanchot, Maurice. "Grève désolée, obscur malaise." In *Qui vive? Autour de Julien Gracq*, 33–8. Paris: José Corti, 1989.

Delahaye, Ernest. "Rimbaud, l'artiste et l'être moral." In *Delahaye, témoin de Rimbaud*, edited by Frédéric Eigeldinger and André Gendre, 29–54. Neuchâtel: Éditions La Baconnière, 1974.

Gracq, Julien. "Entretien avec Jean Carrière." In *Œuvres complètes II*, edited by Bernhild Boie, 1231–73. Paris: Gallimard, 1995.

—. "Liberté grande." Interview by Jean Paget. Recorded in 1969. In *Les Préférences de Julien Gracq – Les Grandes Heures*. Paris: Ina/France Culture/Scam, 2006.

—. "Melanges de textes anciens." NAF 28515 (22), n.d. Fonds Julien Gracq. Archives et Manuscrits, Bibliothèque Nationale de France.

—. "Pourquoi la littérature respire mal." In *Œuvres complètes I*, edited by Bernhild Boie, 857–81. Paris: Gallimard, 1989.

Plazy, Gilles. *Julien Gracq en extrême attente*. Rennes: Part commune, 2006.

Translator's Acknowledgements

Thank you to the editors who have published some of these transla-
tions in magazines: Lee Yew Leong of *Asymptote*, Sarah Coolidge of
Two Lines, Maggie Millner of *The Yale Review*, Bill Pierce of *AGNI*, and
Austin Carder of *Caesura*. I also have Austin to thank for introducing
this project to World Poetry editor Matvei Yankelevich, whom I thank
for his editorial guidance and his belief in this book. Henry Gifford
contributed astute edits to the English text, and Dylan Estruch pro-
vided invaluable insight into some of the more difficult parts of the
French. I am immensely indebted to Bernhild Boie's Pléiade edition
of Gracq's complete works, which has informed this book from be-
ginning to end.

This project started at Yale, where I translated "The Road" for
Alyson Waters's translation class and *Abounding Freedom* for my se-
nior thesis. Many thanks to my former teachers and fellow students
for supporting my work, especially Thomas Connolly, Candace Sko-
rupa, Robyn Creswell, Alice Kaplan, Julia Powers, Thomas Dumont,
David Yaffe-Bellany, Hector Ricardo Hernandez, and the Advanced
Translation class of Spring 2019. Thank you to the Lewis P. Curtis Fel-
lowship and Tristan Perlroth Prize for funding my research in Gracq's
archives at the Bibliothèque Nationale de France, the Bibliothèque
Universitaire d'Angers, and the Bibliothèque Municipale de Nantes.
Special thanks to Jérôme Villeminoz for his patience as I navigated
the world of archival research for the first time.

As always, I am deeply grateful to my family, friends, and partner,
who have supported me throughout the various stages of research,
translating, and editing for this book over the past five years.

And finally, I thank my friend, former teacher, and cherished
mentor Peter Cole, who took a chance on a soft-spoken sophomore
for the coveted last spot in his introductory translation class in 2017.
You taught me the complexities, wonders, and joys of translation,
opening it up as a practice and art that has enriched my experience
of life and literature. I continue to be in awe of your dedication to

and encouragement of your students and their work; no one has supported my intellectual growth as you have. This book would not have existed without you, and I dedicate it to you.

Julien Gracq (1910–2007) was born Louis Poirier. The pen name he eventually adopted is a combination of Julien Sorel, from Stendhal's *The Red and the Black*, and the Gracchi brothers of the Roman Republic. A history and geography teacher for much of his life, Gracq published his first book in 1938, *The Castle of Argol*, which André Breton praised as the first Surrealist novel. In 1951, Gracq won the Prix Goncourt for *The Opposing Shore*, but refused it out of disdain for the literary establishment. He is one of the few writers whose complete works were published during their lifetime by the Bibliothèque de la Pléiade, France's most prestigious collection of classic authors.

Alice Yang is a teacher and translator based in Lyon, France. Her translations have appeared in *Asymptote*, *Two Lines*, *The Yale Review*, and *AGNI*. She studied literature at Yale.

This book was typeset in Apolline, a Renaissance-inspired serif designed by Jean François Porchez for Typofonderie. The cover, designed by Andrew Bourne, is based on the first edition of Gracq's *Liberté grande*, published by Librairie José Corti in 1946. Typeset by Don't Look Now. Printed and bound by BALTO Print in Lithuania.

 **WORLD POETRY**

Marie-Noëlle Agniau
The Escapades
tr. Jesse Hover Amar

Jean-Paul Auxeméry
Selected Poems
tr. Nathaniel Tarn

Boethius
*The Poems from On the Consolation
of Philosophy*
tr. Peter Glassgold

Maria Borio
Transparencies
tr. Danielle Pieratti

Jeannette L. Clariond
Goddesses of Water
tr. Samantha Schnee

Jacques Darras
John Scotus Eriugena at Laon
tr. Richard Sieburth

Mario dell'Arco
Day Lasts Forever: Selected Poems
tr. Marc Alan Di Martino

Olivia Elias
Chaos, Crossing
tr. Kareem James Abu-Zeid

Jerzy Ficowski
Everything I Don't Know
tr. Jennifer Grotz & Piotr Sommer
PEN AWARD FOR POETRY IN TRANSLATION

Antonio Gamoneda
Book of the Cold
tr. Katherine M. Hedeen &
Víctor Rodríguez Núñez

Mireille Gansel
Soul House
tr. Joan Seliger Sidney

Óscar García Sierra
Houston, I'm the problem
tr. Carmen Yus Quintero

Phoebe Giannisi
Homerica
tr. Brian Sneeden

Zuzanna Ginczanka
On Centaurs & Other Poems
tr. Alex Braslavsky

Julien Gracq
Abounding Freedom
tr. Alice Yang

Leeladhar Jagoori
What of the Earth Was Saved
tr. Matt Reeck

*Nakedness Is My End:
Poems from the Greek Anthology*
tr. Edmund Keeley

Jazra Khaleed
The Light That Burns Us
ed. Karen Van Dyck

Judith Kiros
O
tr. Kira Josefsson

Dimitra Kotoula
The Slow Horizon That Breathes
tr. Maria Nazos

Maria Laina
Hers
tr. Karen Van Dyck

Maria Laina
Rose Fear
tr. Sarah McCann

Perrin Langda
A Few Microseconds on Earth
tr. Pauline Levy Valensi

Afrizal Malna
Document Shredding Museum
tr. Daniel Owen

Joyce Mansour
In the Glittering Maw: Selected Poems
tr. C. Francis Fisher

Manuel Maples Arce
Stridentist Poems
tr. KM Cascia

Ennio Moltedo
Night
tr. Marguerite Feitlowitz

Meret Oppenheim
*The Loveliest Vowel Empties:
Collected Poems*
tr. Kathleen Heil

Giovanni Pascoli
Last Dream
tr. Geoffrey Brock
RAIZISS/DE PALCHI TRANSLATION AWARD

Gabriel Pomerand
Saint Ghetto of the Loans
tr. Michael Kasper &
Bhamati Viswanathan

Rainer Maria Rilke
Where the Paths Do Not Go
tr. Burton Pike

Elisabeth Rynell
Night Talks
tr. Rika Lesser

Waly Salomão
Border Fare
tr. Maryam Monalisa Gharavi

George Sarantaris
Abyss and Song: Selected Poems
tr. Pria Louka

George Seferis
Book of Exercises II
tr. Jennifer R. Kellogg

Seo Jung Hak
The Cheapest France in Town
tr. Megan Sungyoon

Ardengo Soffici
Simultaneities & Lyric Chemisms
tr. Olivia E. Sears

Paul Verlaine
Before Wisdom: The Early Poems
tr. Keith Waldrop & K.A. Hays

Witold Wirpsza
Apotheosis of Music
tr. Frank L. Vigoda

Uljana Wolf
kochanie, today i bought bread
tr. Greg Nissan

Ye Lijun
My Mountain Country
tr. Fiona Sze-Lorrain

Verónica Zondek
Cold Fire
tr. Katherine Silver